The International Garage Sale

THE
International
Garage Sale

Stefan Kanfer

W · W · NORTON & COMPANY

NEW YORK · LONDON

The text of this book is composed in Janson, with display type set in
Benguiat. Composition and manufacturing by The Haddon Craftsmen, Inc.
Book design by Winston Potter.

First Edition

Library of Congress Cataloging in Publication Data

Kanfer, Stefan.
    The international garage sale.

    I. Title.
PS3561.A472I5   1985   813'.54   84-29567

ISBN 0-393-01986-1

W. W. Norton & Company, Inc., 500 Fifth Avenue, New York, N. Y. 10110
W. W. Norton & Company Ltd., 37 Great Russell Street, London WC1B 3NU

1 2 3 4 5 6 7 8 9 0

for Jess Korman

We must make sure that its work is fruitful,
that it is a reality and not a sham, that
it is a force for action and not merely a
frothing of words, that it is a true temple
of peace, in which the shields of many nations
can some day be hung and not merely a cockpit
in a Tower of Babel.

WINSTON CHURCHILL

The International Garage Sale

1

The rifle was real; it was the triggerman who looked like a toy. He had been a clown once, part of a troupe called the Lilliputians. In those days his size was an asset: audiences never forgot him. Radicalized, he found his height a liability: the secret police remembered him. Rumpelstiltzkin, Satan's Shrimp, the Mad Mosquito as the Wanted posters had it, was forced into exile along with his shotgun. For several years he moped in mountain retreats, waiting for an occupation that might combine his two favorite roles: the killer and the fool. This year the Victorious Revolution had granted it to him; he was flying to New York to become a diplomat.

All this was confided to the tall man in the next seat, but the Lilliputian's accent was opaque, and he was drunk. Alec Lessing only understood the part about the circus. The rest of the time he slept and read and worried. Mostly Alec worried. Like all journalists, he had a talent for it. His gaze remained inward until he cleared customs. Once outside, Alec looked up and saw an emir's harem loaded into three black limousines as gross and indifferent as eunuchs. A fourth car, larger than a hearse, was reserved for the royal majesty and a senator. Beethoven's *Grosse Fugue* wafted flawlessly from a back seat. Alec stopped to listen. The Lilliputian shrugged his little shoulders and moved on.

"Now *that* is what Ah call steereo," the senator boomed. He looked back at four weary, accommodating gentlemen in dinner jackets. These were the members of the Vienna String Quartet, earnestly fiddling away to please their host.

"Live music. So much better than FM," the emir replied. "No needle scratch. No tape hiss."

New York glittered malignantly in the early dark.

Alec went back inside the terminal building. He felt in his pockets for some change. Among all the foreign tin and silver there was a single American quarter. The *bureau de change* downstairs had long lines. Like a prisoner allowed one call to the outside he stood before the telephone, pondering the arrangement of numbers on the pushbutton dial. Azie would be asleep. Laura would probably be in her darkroom. A call, provided she was in, would mean three minutes of acrimony. Rose . . . As the coin dropped in the slot Alec felt a sudden tugging of his roots and called his parents' home.

"This is the Wizard speaking," said his father.

"Pop?"

"Take an ordinary boiled peeled egg."

"Pop."

"Ask your audience to put the egg all the way into an ordinary orange juice bottle without breaking it."

"*Pop!*"

"After they fail, *you* take the egg—but first throw a lighted match into the bottle. As the flame uses up the oxygen it will create a vacuum and pull the egg gently in. Presto! Thank you for calling Dial-A-Trick. This is the Wizard speaking. Take an ordinary boiled peeled . . ."

Alec hung up. Long past the age of Social Security, the old con man was still fleecing the sheep. Meantime, Alec had lost his quarter. He chanced a little Belgian slug usable in a Brussels amusement park. It clanked ominously but produced a dial tone. He tried his father's private number.

"This is Josiah Lessing, the Wizard."
"Pop?"
"Alec!"
"Yes."
"Where?"
"JFK."
"Car?"
"No."
"Lift?"
"Thanks."
"Terminal?"
"Sabena."
"Upper?"
"Lower."
"Over."
"Out."
Click.

It was the old man'a routine, adapted by Alec and, later, by his friends. No more than one word was allowed per exchange, and they tried for monosyllables. Phone Ping-Pong they called it, but it had not begun as a game. Old Lessing hated telephones. He needed eye contact. All of his garrulity was saved for audiences. Alec was an audience of one as he sat in the front seat, as the station wagon caromed through Queens potholes, as he followed the Wizard up the stairs of a brick semi-attached Jackson Heights home, as he sat before a noisy fireplace.

"Imagine." The old man's face glowed with the solidity and hue of a mahogany sideboard. A halo of white hair gave him the appearance of a sage, further encouraged by an intonation reminiscent of Frank Morgan as Oz. "In the sunset years, magic enjoys a renaissance. And I, with decades of experience and high ethical standards, can steal the eyeteeth from the yokels all over again. No more three-card monte on street corners."

Logs continued to hiss on the hearth although it was

seventy-two degrees outside. The air-conditioner was turned to Frigi-Cool. For Josiah Lessing appearances were not illusory; they were life.

"I'm proud of you. Proud," said the Wizard when they had settled back in rocking chairs, swirling brandy around in glasses.

"Joe? It's late." At the doorway, a voluminous woman was circling her cheeks with rouge to match the dye of her magenta hair.

"Soon, my blossom," he wheezed. "Soon. This is Titania, my cohort. Titania, my son Alec."

"Oh." The redhead withdrew.

"Shy," the old man explained.

"About a hundred dollars shy," said Alec.

"Same old Alec."

"Same old Wizard."

"Yes. Well. Quite. Where was I? Proud. Every time I see you on TV. On the Sony you look a little green and worn. But on the Zenith you look hale. How do you feel?"

"Like the Sony."

"Jet lag is all. Ah, how your mother would have beamed if she could see you now." He rolled his eyes skyward. "Only she's in Brazil. I got a postcard."

The old man stirred the coals.

"She's searching for the original Amazon tribe. Wants to join them, learn how to organize against a sexist society. Probably wind up as their chief. If she's not eaten. So. What would you be doing in the States?"

"I don't know. The network summoned me."

"Good news?"

"I don't think so. Anyway I'm thinking about going back to teaching."

"Forget it. How many residuals do you get at Princeton? TV is where the action is. From one Merv Griffin I got sixteen club dates."

"Pop, I don't want club dates."

"Do you want to see some new card tricks?"

"No."

He was shown five. The Wizard did the Cup and Balls, the Vanishing Banana, the Transposed Duck, the Surprising Noodle, and the Hat That Pees Like a Dog.

The world blurred and gave way to Calvados, flames, and morning. When Alec awoke he was in his old room with a mouth reminiscent of a hamster nest and indistinct memories of his father's nonstop chatter, the redhead's contralto giggle, and a revue of cards, handkerchiefs, and brass rings. Magic. He loathed the word. It summoned up a childhood on the road. Years in New York hanging around conjurors' stores and clamorous delicatessens, the margins of show business. Watching his father astound the hicks with sleight of hand and misdirection. Sometimes Alec provided the misdirection, mugging at the other end of the stage. Sometimes his mother came out in brassy spangled tights, holding pigeons. But usually it was some assistant with tapered legs, or bleached hair that shimmered like gold in the pinspot, or a great balcony, like the redhead's.

Early on he had fled the primary colors and noise. School became his refuge: a reversal of the American boyhood forever denied him. He lived in the stacks of nonfiction: history, biography, anecdote. When he graduated he crossed over the line between the seats and the desk to become a professor. The academy with its chalky rooms, its pale frowning undergraduates, was antidote and salvation.

Until the talk show at Princeton Junction. The local station had scarcely enough watts to fuel a flashlight. He appeared unwillingly, as part of a panel. The moderator, a thin, motorized feminist, drew him out like a typewriter ribbon. He unspooled with great fluency. He told stories from Tacitus, remembered Freud's favorite joke: "A wife is like an umbrella; sooner or later one takes a cab," sang the last verse of *Finnegans Wake,* and cited the Bible on matters of insomnia and sex.

In that modest pond he was a sensation. Letters and calls followed. He was a guest again, then offered a fifteen-minute show on popular culture. A commuting officer from the network caught him one afternoon. Word got around. Alec went to town for interviews and came back with an offer to do theater and film reviews on the 6:30 news. "Talking heads," he told Laura, as Azie banged her spoon on the high chair. "Who needs it? I'll have to give up everything I love." Starting with the classroom. But he had never truly loved the routine, and he had choked on the chalk dust. At school, the world was always outside, awaiting the young. Professors never graduated.

That May, a junior who had cut his hair Mohawk-style and painted his spavined body to resemble an American flag streaked across the campus, charged into Alec's classroom, and inscribed a quote on the blackboard:

> History occurs twice—the first time as tragedy,
> the second as farce.

It was signed: *Karl Marx.*

Alec picked up the eraser and then set it down slowly. The boy, high on self-regard and hash, had no comprehension of what he had written. He had merely liked the sound of it. In the end, that was the trouble with the academy. You spent the winter teaching them texts, and in the spring all they cared for were slogans. What did they know of tragedy? When had they seen farce? Alec left the cleanup to the next professor or the custodian or a more committed Maoist and walked over the familiar chalky doorsill for the last time.

He was soon to forsake a lot more than teaching: scholarship, the alternate serenity and fervor of campus life,

Laura, Azie, friends, pieces of himself. At the network the hours grew unpredictable, and his wife quickly tired of the commute to see idiot Broadway pastiches, English conflicts of ethics versus instinct, and comedies of failing middle-class expectations. She could get all that, she said, without leaving the living room.

When the shot at Correspondent opened in London, it was used as a hinge to swing open the emergency exit. There were other hinges: Tears, accusations, some of them true, acknowledgment of faded affinity. Lawyers. London beckoned like a garden. The promise of a return home every three months was postponed, then canceled. Assignment followed assignment; he became a familiar jittery image on the home screen. Lately he had been afflicted by the hot, merciless lights, the night flights, the banal, forced question: "We have only thirty seconds left, General: What went wrong?" He had begun to get vague during interviews, and he had been 100 percent wrong in his prognostications. A death wish, maybe. He retreated once more into books. This time he bought Pelicans and Penguins in airport stalls, reminders of the old clothbound volumes that were now stacked in this room, his old retreat, the shelves constructed like a fortress after the acrimonious split with Laura.

He took down a volume from the headboard shelf: *The Complete Works of Halifax*, an old favorite. Alec had once done a thesis on George Savile, Marquess, several oceans and hundreds of assignments before, when his notion of the world was derived from textbooks.

The volume cracked when he opened it; there were water blisters on the margins, souvenirs of the times he had read it in the bathtub. The inscription on the flyleaf was blurred: *To Professor Lessing with gratitude and admiration, Wanda Preiss.* Wanda. Fourth row, second seat. That came back, and parts of the body. She had married a physics major, he remembered, a boy with a beard and glasses and a burgeoning stomach, a Burl Ives type. Fifth row, second seat. Ivan somebody. Halifax beckoned from the stained page:

Folly is often more cruel in the consequence than malice can be in the intent.

"Your awfice cawled."

Titania stood in the doorway erupting from her housecoat. The face, unmarked by thought, humor, or rouge, widened and contracted at the temples as she chewed sugarless gum.

"They want you to cawl back. Chop-chop."

"Where's my father?"

"The Wizard? Downtown. He'll be back on the weekend, he said to tell you."

"Downtown takes three days?"

"Not downtown here. Downtown Vegas. He's doing club dates."

"Don't you travel with him?"

"No. I only do stage stuff where the yuks can ogle my jugs. This is strictly closeup effects. Cards, coins, stuff like that. Besides, I got a regular job in Soho."

She stayed at the doorway. Alec returned to his book. She remained, chewing gum metronomically. He turned back to her.

"Doing what?" he asked.

"I'm sort of a hostess. In an alley. Me and another girl. Mostly S and M. She whips me and then I walk over her with spike heels. Except it's all fake: a sponge rubber whip and I walk very soft. You wanna come down and catch the act sometime?"

"Absolutely. What do you call yourselves?"

"The Diplomats."

She popped another bubble and vanished. Her scent, Dayglo for the nose, remained. Alec turned on the Sony. The sound was off. An image jittered on the screen: some ballplayer pushing razor blades. Alec reached for the volume control and froze. The images were of wreckage: the remnants of a car, strewn across Fifty-second Street. Police picked through the smoking iron. A burst water main, Alec guessed, or a gas explosion. Then he saw him in the upper right corner of the screen: the Lilliputian stood with a small crowd of onlookers. Alec turned up the sound. The emir appeared, shaking his head. He had accepted the senator's kind invitation for dinner. He and his bodyguards had debarked at the Four Seasons, and the car had just gone up the street when they heard "a horrific crack, like that of doom." "Poor Achmed," he kept saying.

The emir was reminded that he had missed death for the fifth time this year. The information was met with a shrug. "I am," he said, "one lucky potentate. My chauffeur was not so fortunate. When the assassins are found they will receive the fate of all radical anarchist rebels. They will be flogged in the marketplace, welted by the knout, slashed by the scimitar, seared by the sun, smeared with honey and fed to the fire ants, like all the others."

"Who could have done such a thing?" the newsman demanded.

"I have no idea," the emir said mildly. "I am a progressive, peace-loving man."

A sunburned, sweating associate in a dark business suit intervened. Below him on screen appeared the identification: *Hamid Daladan.* "It is clearly a case of mistaken identity," he said. "Chicago thugs. The Mafia. Street gangs. To the Western eye, all caliphs look alike."

As Daladan spoke, the camera panned through the

crowd, but by that time the Lilliputian had vanished.

The image of the little man bothered Alec, but other thoughts soon crowded it out. He was still pondering the demands of child support and unemployment benefits as he entered the Narcissus, a new restaurant on the roof of the network building. Here, along the archipelago of white tablecloths, under the insect noise of egos rubbing against deals, employees and guests stole quick looks at themselves in a wall of mirrors and ordered health foods. These were arranged on the left side of the menu; on the right, instead of prices, were listed the nutritive values of the day's entrees:

Mock Turkey
(Small curd cottage cheese,
chopped organic almonds,
salt substitute, Norwegian
cod liver oil, kelp.)

Vitamins A, B, B$_2$, B$_{12}$,
D, Niacinamide, pantothenic
acid, trace cobalt, copper,
iron, iodine.

No alcohol was permitted, except for:

White California Wine

Vitamin C, trace copper,
magnesium.

Alec recognized some of the bobbing, lunching heads; most were strangers, moodily chewing their mung bean sprouts like cud. The restaurant was the idea of General Wolfe, who dined there occasionally. He was eating now, chomping on a mock hamburger and reading a three-page treatment of *Gulliver's Travels*, proposed by the programming department as a mini-series. Long ago, even before he had become president and chief stockholder of the network, the General had formed his theory of the world's evil. Caligula, Genghis Khan, Napoleon, Hitler, Stalin, Idi Amin had all risen from one source: sugar. Excessive sucrose could drive men mad, cause them to go to war, dissolve their loyalties, and tyrannize their children. It had triggered revolutions and toppled dynasties; it lay at the

root of female depression, of male impotence, of ir-
regularity, varicose veins, schizophrenia, gallstones, dan-
druff. And yet in every restaurant in the country the poison
lay in miniature sandbags, in glass and metal containers,
free for the taking. The General and his Anti-Sugar Council had campaigned long and hard; it had cost his stations
advertising, but such was his incorruptibility that he never
lowered his voice. No sugar was allowed in his private
restaurant and he attributed his health and that of his staff
—there had been only one thrombosis in the last fiscal
quarter—to his dietary restrictions. General Wolfe's own
flawless electrocardiogram and low blood pressure were
mute evidence that, although overweight, his sugar-free
body was ageless. He did not stir that body or betray any
sign of recognition as his employee, Alec Lessing, walked
by. The news editor, D. M. Grambling, by way of welcome, waved a forkful of alfalfa five tables away. Alec warily joined him.

Grambling looked worn beneath his nut-brown toupee and Caribbean tan. "Goddam gerbil food," he complained *sotto voce.* "I'm fifty-six years old, for Chrissake. I
should be allowed a coronary every once in a while if I
want. Jesus." But he kept eating and forcing a smile, in case
the General glanced his way. "Help yourself, Professor."
He waved at the greenery.

Alec was not hungry. Actually he was nauseous. But
he poured some wine.

"I know I should save this for dessert," Grambling
began, "but I have to go back and edit a rape in the Bronx."

"Don't let me keep you."

"The point is, you're a true gentleman."

"Thank you," Alec replied, disarmed.

"What I don't need."

"Pardon?"

"Is gentlemen. You're the type that feels he's intruding if he takes the back off a watch. Also, if it was six o'clock, you couldn't predict nighttime. Fact."

"Well, I—"

"You say the linthead premier is resigning, he goes on the fucking satellite to tell the world he's staying on. Two schvoogies in Nairobi? You say nobody cares, they win the Nobel. We want some art happenings, you give us footage on what's-his-face."

"William Blake. I thought it looked good in color."

"So does an oil spill. You know the rule on prime time. Culture is for Sunday afternoon, after the cartoons and before the kickoff."

Grambling ruminated in silence. When it grew unbearable, Alec said, "You want me to say it for you?"

"Say what?"

"I'm fired."

"Ha! I wish. Only, the AFTRA contract comes up next month and the General sent a memo. No more dismissals until rerun time. But I *am* sending you where you belong."

Alec had brief, unedited visions of Arctic tundra, icicles forming on the end of his nose; or Uganda, his head on a pikestaff held aloft by shouting soldiers with tribal scars; an official government protest, delivered through the Ghanaian ambassador; the Alec Lessing memorial scholarship fund . . . He would surely have to quit now, go back to school. It was doubtful that Princeton would have him. He had forsworn teaching without a backward glance. Jobs were scarce in the academy; he had read about it somewhere. Or had he said it himself on the air?

"I'm sending you to the WEB," Grambling told him.

"The which?"

"The WEB, the World Body. Exile. The pits. Help yourself. I got work to do."

But as Grambling prepared to leave, an unusual incident occurred. The massive shaved head loomed over the table and caught the light. "Mind if I join you? Unless it's private? I thought not."

General Wolfe settled in like a fog. Grambling never needed to worry about the proper replies to his chief. The General always answered his own interrogations before allowing a reply.

"Don't let me interrupt," he said. "I believe in delegating authority. Where are you sending . . . Albert Lessing, isn't it?—I thought so."

"Yes."

"Not far away, I hope? Good."

"Nearby, General."

"It may surprise you, Alfred, but I'm an internationalist. I believe in travel. Every year I go on a fact-finding trip to Africa and the Middle East or China. Last year I saw a panda." The General glowed. Grambling reflected his light. Alec morosely drained his glass. "Have you read *Gulliver's Travels*?" asked the chief executive. "We all have."

A chorus of nods.

"We may do it in four successive nights. Everybody thinks it's just about a giant and little people. But there are other adventures. We could do one of them from the point of view of the horse. What do you think? Fascinating."

"Compelling," Grambling agreed.

"What Gulliver is all about, really, is travel. If we stress that, we can get an airline to underwrite the whole thing."

"Or possibly a racetrack," Alec offered.

"What?"

"For the horse episode, I mean."

Grambling sat ready to pounce. But the General missed whatever salt was in Alec's offering. "No, we're looking for somebody to pick up the whole package," he said. "The point is, everyone's interested in foreign countries, different faces, strange languages and people. That's why . . . you haven't been assigned yet? No."

"No," Grambling assured him hastily.

"I don't know much about your work, Alden, but my wife says your chin comes over as cleft. Women constitute how much of the audience? A lot."

"Sixty-three percent," Grambling announced.

"Exactly. We need a good chin on international news."

. . . Not far from this restaurant the green freshmen were gathering in the commons, arguing about power, swimming upstream to their instructors, spawning clutches of theses. . . . Alec wondered if Unemployment could get him through until fall. Then, perhaps at Bennington . . .

"You need to trade up," General Wolfe told Alec. "To the WEB."

"The WEB," Grambling repeated numbly.

"The last man who was at the World Body—"

"Ellenbogen," Grambling supplied the name.

"Exactly. We had to let Ellenbogen go. We found he was writing a book. You're not writing a book, are you, Allen? Certainly not."

"Me? No."

"Fine. It's been my experience that a man who's writing a book is not working."

"Just before you came by I was telling Alec about the WEB," Grambling began.

But the General had already risen. "Don't get up," he said. Nevertheless, the men rose. Grambling watched the broad back of his chief as it made its way out of the Narcissus, through ranks of fawning waiters and network personnel.

"Well," said Alec after a period of dead air. "Everybody's happy, it looks like."

"Jesus, *Gulliver's Travels,*" Grambling said to his nut-burger.

Laura's place was new. The furniture was different. His ex-wife was a little thinner and there were lines of strain around her mouth, deepened perhaps by Alec's appearance.

"Hello." He gave her a bunch of white chrysanthemums and tried to kiss her but Laura adroitly took the blossoms and ducked his face.

He nodded, mostly to himself, and came in.

"Where's Azie?"

"Rehearsing. She's in the Calhoun pageant. They're doing the Tonight Show. She plays Sammy Davis Jr."

"Wouldn't it be better if they got a black to play him?"

"There's only one black in the class. And she wanted to play Johnny Carson."

They smiled in silence, drinking Riesling and occasionally meeting each other's eyes.

"So," Laura said after a while. "Did they fire you?"

"No, they gave me a promotion."

"Typical."

"At least they think it's a promotion. I'm going to be the correspondent at the WEB."

"What web?"

"That's what they call it. The World Body."

"Oh."

"I'll be in town from now on."

"Lucky me."

"Look at it this way: the checks will be five thousand miles closer."

The buzzer rang. Laura got up and pressed a buzzer in the kitchen. While she did Alec had a look around. On the Baldwin Acrosonic, the *Notebook of Anna Magdalena Bach* lay open. Too primary for Laura, too advanced for Azie. Probably there was a man by now, although Laura seethed too much for him to have much significance. The apartment betrayed no male signs, no pictures, no pipes, no discernible souvenirs. In the bathroom he saw only two toothbrushes, one large and one small; no stranger stayed here regularly, or else Laura was very, very careful.

He looked up to see Azie at the door. Like a good city child she shut it, turned the bolt, and remembered to put the Fox lock back in place. Then she turned.

"Hello, Daddy," she said in a faraway voice.

"Hello, Azie." Something about her stance told him not to kneel down, as in other times, and open his arms. He saw a bit of makeup still clinging near the light-brown hairline, and another behind her shrimpshell ear.

"How was the show?" he asked.

"Good. Except the orchestra sucked."

"Azie," Laura said between her teeth.

"Sorry," Azie said. The large gray eyes followed her mother until Laura exited into the kitchen.

"But they did suck," she whispered to her father.

"You still have Sammy Davis Jr. behind your ear," Alec told her. She came to him and let him wipe some of it off with his handkerchief. He kissed the top of her head.

"How is school?" he asked. "I mean let's get that out of the way first. And then I won't ask you again until you're forty."

"It's OK. Except for the extra reading." Azie snored ostentatiously and offered him a glance at her notebook: *"Peter: The Myth and the Rabbit. 'Watership Down.' Bugs Bunny as Gadfly."*

"The teacher is very big on rabbits," Alec concluded.

"Mrs. Damon *is* a rabbit. You should see her teeth. She

could eat an apple through a tennis racquet. Are you going
to be here long?"

"Here in New York?"

"No, *here* here. In the apartment."

"I don't think so. Your mother has other plans."

"No she doesn't."

"Yes she does." Laura reentered the living room with
two mugs of coffee. "We have to get you a pair of ballet
slippers."

"I thought you said Tuesday."

"There'll be lots of other times, Azie," Alec assured
her. Laura sat, but Alec remained standing, sipping at his
coffee. "I'm going to be based here in New York. Right up
the street, practically."

"Will you be on the 7:00 news?"

"Sometimes."

"When you were away I used to hope there was a
disaster every night wherever you were."

"Azie . . ."

"So you would be on TV and I could see you." She said
the line over her shoulder and disappeared down the hall.

"Thank you, *Reader's Digest.*" Laura immediately bit
her lip. "I'm sorry," she said. "Azie really meant that. She
still kisses the set when you're on it."

For the first time her voice relented a little and soft-
ened at the corners.

"How are you, Alec?" she asked him. "Really. Everything all right under the hood?"

Before he could reply, Azie yelled from her room:
"They're showing *Bambi* at the Thalia. Would you take
me?"

"Would I? It's my favorite."

"Me too. That and *Death Wish.*"

Alec turned on Laura with a loud, hot whisper: "You
took her to see a movie about violence and killings?"

"I didn't take her. It was on television."

"Even so—"

"I wasn't here," she said between her teeth. "The sitter was a cinema major. Never mind. You wouldn't begin to understand."

After that the air crackled and Alec took his leave as soon as he could. He looked at Laura and Azie as they gathered the mugs and glasses. It would not be easy, raising a child alone, especially one with an independent nature and too much familiarity with the themes of marital discord.

Halifax had worried about *his* daughter:

Whilst you are playing, full of innocence, the spiteful world will bite, except you are guarded by your caution.

How much more spiteful the world seemed now.

He looked at the wall of autographed portraits. Richard Avedon: *To Laura with gratitude.* Bert Stern: *To Laura with love.* Irving Penn: *To Laura with affection.* Everybody loved Laura. Except her husband, toward the end. Why? Because he hated cameras, he used to tell himself. All they did was take; photographers took pictures, they never gave them.

"What are you working on?" he asked her. The work table was filled with snapshots of blue-gray fowl, fledglings, adults, and mottled eggs.

"A children's book. About owls who get separated."

"Making it understandable for kids?"

"For owls."

The work, like the photographer, had deeper focus and contrasts than he had remembered. The lines of birds stretched across the paper like etchings.

Alec kept looking at them, and at Azie. On the way out

he fingered the sheet music on the piano.

"I started playing Bach again," Laura said absently.

"Isn't this too simple?"

"No. The older I get, the better I like simplicity."

The remark had the sting of criticism. Alec puzzled about it for a long time afterward. But somehow he was comforted by the information that it was only Laura and not a visitor who was playing the *Notebook of Anna Magdalena Bach.*

The World Body is housed on some of the most expensive land in the world: fifteen acres overlooking the East River. But it was not always so high-priced. A hundred and fifty years ago the acreage was the home of squatters and small farms and leather-tanning factories whose odor prompted neighbors to call the area by a single name. Wave upon wave of immigrants made it their address. The Germans called it *der Halle de Schweiner Scheisse,* the Hispanics *Salón Plasta Cochina,* the Gaels *Slainfersalieric,* the Italians *Maiale Corridio,* and the English Pigshit Hall.

So it remained until the Blands, a banking family who liked New York but did not inhale, purchased the land for investment. Down went the little refineries, down went Klaus Flugel's brewery, the shacks, and factories; up rose tenements and restaurants and mercantile establishments. Proud of their development, the Blands called it New East.

But when Cotton Bland ran for governor his opponents showed up at rallies with pictures of hogs and worse, and turned his speeches into festivals of humiliation. When M. Armstrong Bland offered to sell New East to the city for a concert hall, a mayoral assistant openly oinked, triggering a scandal that resulted in a new mayor, a private apology, and the cancellation of the sale.

The site fell into its penultimate decay. Opium was peddled in hallways, old men were mugged in daylight; gangs of children roamed the streets breaking shop windows and stealing hubcaps. One winter, E. Morris Bland hired a certified pyromaniac to set fire to the entire district. The residents and shopkeepers were rescued by World War II. All personal plans were canceled or postponed for the duration. When the war ended, the ravaged and victorious nations agreed that global conflict must be ended forevermore. Senator, later Ambassador, Bland, caught by the benign energy of the postwar epoch, offered New East for the proposed World Body. Bulldozers were set to work, tenants relocated, streets torn up, waterfronts redesigned. Late in the '40s, two gleaming professional buildings rose to house the delegations of the countries from all the dry surfaces of the globe, an institution dedicated to the elevation of the human species regardless of race or national origin, and to such broad inarguable causes as freedom from war, prejudice, and disease. Now, as the World Body approached its fifth decade, William Hackett, senior member of the press corps, sat in the press room surveying its newest member and iterating his view of the World Body and its history.

"Welcome," he said, "to Pigshit Hall."

Hackett had the undernourished vulpine face of a television evangelist. An overlay of capillaries and a mouth twitch hinted at secret indulgences. One of them was Stolichnaya vodka. It mixed and blended with his grapefruit juice as the two journalists looked out the windows south to the gleaming hospitals, and across the river to the factory fumes of Queens.

In front of the main building with its green windows staring emptily westward, banners of 183 nations snapped and clanged on long shiny steel poles. They reminded Alec of the periodic table of elements: some were stable and permanent, like sulphur or iron: England or France or his home country. Others were newly made, like Einsteinium or Zimbabwe. And there were the vanished molecules, possessors of what the chemists called half-life: Biafra came to mind.

"On your way up or down, Squire?" Hackett's intonation suggested British schooling.

"I don't know, really. I—"

"My guess is up." He fingered Alec's suit. "Trumbull?"

"Yes."

"Up."

Hackett pulled at the liquid in his paper cup.

"You married?" he persisted.

"I was."

"Me too. Three times. Eight children. We minority groups breed like flies."

"What group is that?"

"Didn't you know? I'm Chinese. I lied about my eyes."

This was followed by wracking laughter indistinguishable from retching. Hackett's face colored from the exertion.

"Alimony put me here," he snuffled. "My trouble is, I always marry them, you see." Tears caught the fluorescent light. "I get a disability check from the government, but it doesn't go far."

He waited for a question but none was forthcoming. A preturnatural shyness on Alec's part, about past injuries.

Hackett sat down. "A war wound. In the Azores. Transport crash. Half my face scarred, burnt beyond recognition. They rebuilt the whole thing. Over a hundred skin grafts."

"It's a remarkable job," Alec assured him. "You can't tell at all."

"No, no, it shows. In the veins, the thick skin. I like my

booze, but not the way it shows in the epidermis. This is all skin off my backside, you see." He brightened. "Can you lend me five until next Monday? I get paid next Monday."

Alec took a five-dollar bill from his wallet and handed it over, a gift, he sensed; an initiation fee.

"No, no, Squire," said Hackett, seizing the money. "I meant five hundred."

"I'm afraid I don't have that kind of—"

"Yes, well, you've got your own alimony. Still, it didn't hurt to ask. One day they'll send me a young man with a trust fund. You want a schedule?"

"What sort of schedule?"

"Of meetings, plenary sessions, things like that."

"Yes, I guess, thank you."

"Well, there isn't any. Best thing to do is root around, ask questions. But not of me. The others."

"Where are the others?"

"Oh, around. Bars, mostly. Assignations. Things like that. Most of them come in about once a week, file a story that never runs, use the phones, and so on."

"Where are they the rest of the time? At the sessions?"

Again Hackett produced fragmented laughter.

"Forgive me," he said finally. "We haven't had a new boy in months. Sessions with girls, yes. Or boys in Abu's case. But sessions at the WEB? No. Hardly. Sessions!" He went back to his fitful mirth. When he stopped shaking, he said, "Been assigned an office yet?"

"No."

"Here, use mine." He took Alec down the dark-blue carpeted hall to a closed door with the name of Hackett's wire service lettered in gold leaf.

"Are you sure?" Alec asked.

"Go ahead. Until you're assigned one. I'm going to be out anyway."

As Hackett showed him the key to the rest room and

the location of telephone banks, a small, cigar-shaped military man knocked and entered without bidding. His uniform was the color of moss and festooned with ribbons and clanking silver and copper medals. The epaulets were orange and green: the colors of the country it represented.

"Colonel Vietor Pakima De Faxe," he shouted. "I have come to present myself to the press. I myself was a journalist. I understand the problems of the deadline. Five minutes to go and no story. I am here to help. You will take down the following paragraphs."

He smiled and the gold that was missing from his medals shone in his mouth. He referred to a group of three-by-five cards in his right hand.

"The government of El Chazade is now in the hands of the freely elected representatives of the Guardia Royale, a group of nine colonels of the army and air force. Former President Juan Garcia-Krauss is under house arrest in the capital city, pending trial for crimes against the state, among them extortion, corruption, treason, and speeding."

He paused. "You are not writing," he said.

"Got an eye for detail, ain't he?" Hackett winked at Alec. "Look here," he said to the officer, "you just have a seat. My friend and I have a small conference to attend. Then I'll come back and get the story. Have part of a cigar? Ashtray's on the desk."

Hackett steered Alec back to the press room.

"Typical oligarch," he confided. "Has a toothache, thinks the whole world's in pain. I'll take care of it. You relax in here."

Alec sat in silence, examining brochures about the World Body, sharpening pencils, and reading the advertisements for movies in the *Times*. It was as quiet as a Christian Science reading room. After a while he grew curious and went back to Hackett's office. The two men were still there; he could hear voices.

"Fascinating, Colonel, fascinating. There's definitely a story in it. *If* I can grease the right palms. Editors, publishers, the like."

"How much is the cost of such grease?"

"Always liked the military. Very direct. Bit of a war hero myself, Colonel. Wounded in Malta. A land mine. Just like in *The Sun Also Rises: 'Que malfortuna.* You have given more than your life.' No more women, I thought. But the doctors fashioned a new one, out of plastic and skin grafts. Trouble is, I had only two choices—tumescence or not. Goes without saying which I chose. Drives the ladies mad. Had five wives, nine children. Artificial insemination. From myself. Peculiar; in several textbooks, actually. But sad, sad. I always marry them, you see."

"How much is the cost of such grease?"

"Fifteen hundred?"

"Pesetas or dollars?"

"Dollars, always dollars."

"Cash or check?"

"Cash."

There was some shuffling and rustling of paper.

"Not here, you wombat," Hackett's voice protested. "I'll show you where."

Squeaks of chairs were followed by outraged mumbles and mollifying whispers.

Alec ducked back into the press room until the two men passed down the hall, the colonel's speech punctuated by Hackett's reassurances.

Alec returned to Hackett's office. He sat there watching the East River. He sharpened pencils. He called the numbers for time, for weather, for traffic conditions, although he could see the traditional embolisms of the East River Drive as rush hour approached. He called Dial-A-Joke:

"First cannibal is reading *People* magazine. Second cannibal says, 'Hey, is that dehydrated stuff any good?' "

And he read Halifax. The Marquess stared out at him from the frontispiece, wig cascading in the dictated ringlets, lace bunched at the throat. But the face signaled forbearance, and the sharp black eyes were in no mood for flattery or indulgence:

It is the fools and the knaves that make the wheels of the World turn. They *are* the World; those few who have the sense of honesty sneak up and go down single, but never go in herds.

And here he was in a herd; part of the electronic paparazzi, the keyhole starers. Who was it saw the press as sharks swimming after an ocean liner from which garbage was thrown, and now and then a genuine human body?

It was six now; maybe his friend Crow was home. As Alec dialed, a large squat lady in white charged in, bearing a galvanized-iron pail and a mop and broom.

"You one dirty man," she said.

"This is not really my office," Alec began. "I—"

"You very dirty man." She clanged the pail for emphasis. "All the time you mek mess, I clean up. Ashtrays, wastebaskets, floor. Even ceiling."

Alec followed her eyes skyward. The acoustic ceiling was marred by inverted pencils stuck in the tiles, like stalactites.

"But dis!" she continued. "Dis too much. Come." He followed her down the hall to the press room. She stopped before a large canvas receptacle on wheels. "I empty wastebasket in here," she explained furiously. "Now see what happens." Alec came over and looked. There was a small man inside, resting on thousands of discarded memos. He was wearing a dark blue suit and white shirt and no tie. His eyes were closed and he was breathing evenly.

"I no throw away man," the cleaning lady insisted.

"No, of course not."

"American?"

"Me? Yes. I think he's just sleeping, actually," Alec said. "Why don't you let me—"

"Waste gas, waste food, waste paper. Now waste man. Good for years yet. You throw away. American. Feh!"

She waddled off, muttering in Balto-Slavik.

Alec reached in a hand and tried to stir the snoring figure. Fumes of stale bourbon drifted up.

"I forgot to tell you about Pandit. He always sleeps it off in the basket." Hackett had come back unannounced. "Reminds him of home. Don't bother to wake him up, Squire. He'll only start talking about women. Very common person, Pandit. Like a light bulb: on or off."

Hackett departed. Alec stood for another moment, considering the little man and the World Body and New York. He dialed Crow and began another Ping-Pong game.

"Hello?"

"Hello."

"Alec?"

"Yes."

"Home?"

"Right."

"Drink?"

"Now?"

"Sure."

"Where?"

"Clark's?"

"Mobbed."

"Billy's?"

"Fine."
"Six?"
"Thirty."
"Done."

Billy's was also mobbed, but there was room at the bar. Crow was already there, fresh from his sportscast, reading the racing results in the *Afternoon Paper*. There was no irony in his name; he looked like a bird. The black hair was abundant but undisciplined, and the face was long and thin and curious, like his head, like the rest of him. Crow kept his raincoat on while he drank. It matched his black turtleneck and trousers.

"Are you happy, that's the point," Crow began.

"Who the hell is happy?"

"You're not, then."

"I don't know. At least I'm home."

"Staying where?"

"Any place, no place."

"And that's home?"

"I mean New York. Near Azie."

"You want to borrow Ellen's? I've got the key."

"Crow, how do you stay friends with your ex-wife?"

"Ah, well, we were kids when we married. And she's a very understanding person. And she's out of town and somebody's got to water the plants and feed the cats. I was right, by the way. She's bestial."

Alec expressed sorrow to hear it.

"If she had left me for another man," Crow told him, "I could be hurt, angry. Lost. But when your wife leaves you for a horse, how are you supposed to feel? There are no books on the subject. I'm a pioneer."

Crow looked at his palms.

"Anyway, I'm off soon." Crow brightened. "New assignment. Hazards, night missions. Treachery, backstabbing. Intrigues."

"Where?"

"Marriage. I'm getting married again. Did I tell you that?"

"No."

"Well, I am."

"Who to?"

"I don't really know. But I'm tired of living alone, waking up with no one to talk to. I need a wife in the mornings. I'm serially monogamous."

"Breakfast cereally monogamous anyway."

"What? Oh. Yes." Crow forced a smile. "Same old Alec."

Same old Alec. His father had said that, his ex-wife had implied it; now his friend repeated it. But he felt different. Out of place, no longer quite of the city, perhaps even of the country. The feeling on this pleasant soupy evening was ominous. Why, he couldn't say. Maybe it was just a reentry problem. Perhaps it was the WEB. Something that was said or not said wrinkled his brain. He drank and forgot it. Later Crow went prowling the singles bars in search of a wife, the only man on the entire island of Manhattan to do so. Invited along, Alec refused. Crow gave him the keys to his own apartment and Alec walked to Seventy-third Street and up the stairs. He took the spare room, turned on channel 29, and started fading out as *The Third Man* unreeled.

"What is it?" Joseph Cotten inquired.

"It's only the main sewer," the sergeant told him. "Smells sweet, don't it?"

"I've been a fool," Trevor Howard said. "We should have dug deeper than a grave."

Alec did not see the next scene. He fell asleep and

dreamed the rest of the film. Orson Welles reminded him of the emir. There were some scenes of pursuit in sewers, and sometimes he was the pursuer, and sometimes the pursued. His heart accelerated. He saw seven fat oil wells devouring seven lean ones. He awoke to a blank cycloptic screen and the voices of Crow and a singing companion. She had a small, true voice but the notes wavered. There was more giggling, followed by whispers. Crow barged into the spare room.

"Only woman there without two heads," he explained thickly. "Needs alarm clock. Appointment tomorrow at nine." He found an old clock and wound it, shook it at his ear, failed to hear ticking, and sat down heavily on a stool. He pried off the back with a key, noisily refusing aid. "Go on sleeping," he said. The back of the clock fell off with a sharp metallic clatter.

Crow looked inside at the gears and the mainspring. He reached in and drew out a mangled roach. "No wonder it doesn't work," he told Alec tragically. "The engineer is dead."

He waited for his head to clear. "Look at this face," he remarked, half to the mirror, half to his listener. "Why do they pay it all this money? Because its eyes are close together. Wide eyes, no television. Close eyes, brown, sports. Medium eyes, blue, anchorman. You know what my real name is?"

"Yes." Alec said.

"Rosario Baravelli. The kind of name they use to cover block parties. Circuses. So I changed it to what the kids used to call me at P.S. 89, 'Crow.' I'm a celebrity. I can get a good table at Elaine's. Fourteen-year-old jocks stop me on the street to talk about soccer."

A feminine voice beckoned to him from the other room. But Crow continued: "You know what the trouble is, Alec? Elaine's is noisy. I don't want to talk to kids about

the Tampa Bay Rowdies. You know what I want to do?"
"Yes."
"I want to teach. Quietly somewhere. Away from road
trips and interviews with cruiserweights. I want to retire
while I'm young and feel good all the time. You got any
aspirin?"
"It's your house," Alec reminded him. "Listen, Crow:
you won't remember any of this in the morning, but school
is where I came from. Teaching's not for people like us.
Our pulses are too rapid."
"I'm tired of the fast lane. I want everything *andante.*"
He tried to stand. "When you're out of town and you
see a war memorial outside the village courthouse, don't
you read all the names with gold stars?"
"I try to, yes, but—"
"There isn't time, right? There never is. That's what
I want. Time to read the gold stars." He clumped back to
his bridal candidate.
Moaning, shifting of furniture, and suppressed laughter murdered sleep. Alec tried to read but the meanings hid
themselves behind the words, like peas under shells. The
only program visible on the screen at that hour was some
UHF channel broadcasting a pornographic cooking class.
Alec turned it off and watched the ceiling, listening to his
unquiet heart. When the rays of morning crept around the
shade, and the city cleared its throat and Alec decided to
remain awake, sensitive to every sound and impulse in this
tormented place, to become reacquainted with the things
that had formed him: when he had decided to forsake even
a nap, he blinked too slowly and the nap took him.

2

There was no need to go anywhere. A wall of television monitors brought the world to Grambling. He sat in a large dark control room running his hands through his toupee and watching catastrophe spin from reels of videotape. Wherever there was carrion, the Network was on location.

It was Saturday, and most of the city was at play. Not the news staff. Alec had been summoned from his sleep at 6:00 A.M. He had cancelled his boat ride on the Hudson with Azie. There were more than the customary recriminations from Laura, and Azie's stoical voice had tears in it. Now he sat in a black swivel chair, shifting miserably left and right, watching alternate screens as the miseries presented themselves.

Scarcely two hours ago, reported the Mideast correspondent, Yousef the Lookout noticed a peculiar series of wobbles massed on the horizon. At first he attributed the sight to a mirage, but never before had optical illusions produced the rumble of heavy metal. Tanks were visible within twenty minutes. He released a single flare into the cerulean sky, but whether it was observed he never knew. By the time Yousef checked the horizon again troops of the emir were upon him.

At noon, Paris noted, towers of the Gallimar observatory picked up a shower of metal foil in their radar screens.

Within the next quarter hour radio signals were jammed throughout the Distant Early Warning Line of NATO.

Seconds later, troops of India and the People's Republic of China clashed at a remote outpost in Nepal. In the Transvaal, white troops were fired upon by guerrillas of the Orbu tribe. There was splendid color footage, with red predominant. Toward sunset, the Italian government fell, and Cuban soldiers in fatigues were observed on patrol in the forests outside Brasilia.

At the same hour, men of two U.S. infantry divisions concluded their war games and boarded transport planes for the Azores and Taiwan. History felt immediate; apocalypse beckoned. Still, those who had taught the lessons of the past were not yet ready for awe. They recalled other conflagrations, other lands where barbarians had run salt into the earth and left not even an animal alive, and still civilization had survived. Plague and fire had not kept Halifax from worrying about his family:

Love is presently out of breath when it is to travel uphill from the children to the parents.

The child was the only center Alec had now, and she blocked his view of the world. When the lunch break finally came, he searched for an apartment. He had no time to find what he really wanted, something spacious and close to Azie, so he settled for a sublet on Riverside Drive with furniture that smelled of cats.

At the WEB, office phones rang in various keys. But except for Hackett, no one was present. Alec toured the assembly rooms; there were meetings in all of them.

Voices came from a small auditorium with leather-covered doors. Alec looked in.

"My God," a delegate from Ghana was saying. "Everything at once. This could mean the collapse of civilization."

"Ah," said the man in the burnoose warmly, rubbing his hands. "But can we bank on it?"

On another floor in a larger room, delegates from sixteen countries ringed a large dais. Each of them had a microphone and from time to time a chairman would call upon them to speak. Alec picked up a set of earphones and dialed. Simultaneous translators spoke in French, then, as he turned a dial, in Spanish, Chinese and English.

". . . The Zionist hordes who have been responsible for the dissolution of the legitimate rights—"

". . . The insatiable imperialist demands of the Soviet Socialist Republics—"

". . . It is not Cuba that is exporting revolution, it is the United States that is supporting counterrevolution—"

". . . Colonialist powers are in a poor position to criticize those who wish to contain certain dangerous groups without *habeas corpus*. This is purely an internal matter—"

"May I help you?" It was the man from the oversized wastebasket. Today he was erect and brightly lit. "You are from the press?"

"Yes." Alec showed his card.

The man was dressed in a blue suit, darker than the one of last week. He had on a white bow tie badly tied and a blue shirt. His skin was the color of sandalwood and his teeth shone in contrast.

"Ram Pandit," he said by way of introduction. "Translator. Oh my goodness, one is getting very confused after two hours in there. I speak nine languages. What are we talking now?"

"English."

"Ah! English. My favorite. Shakespeare, Milton, Benny Hill—"

Alec held up his hands in an attempt to brake Pandit. "I'm new. Something's going on, something I don't understand. Something unspoken. You've worked here awhile."

"Eight years."

"Well? And?"

"Like you I have the sense that there are things moving below the surface. Like bodies under sheets. Something fascinating yet at the same time dirty."

"But what?"

"My friend, let us talk about something more important than international intrigue."

"Pandit, this could be a matter of human survival. What could be more important than that?"

"Legs. I myself prefer long thin ones. Some men prefer breasts. Not me. A breast leads nowhere. Whereas the leg—"

Alec moved on. Pandit followed him for a while, yapping at his heels: "You are green. You think in grandiose terms: a great international forum, momentous decisions. This is not the path of wisdom. The way of enlightenment is yoga. The eternal OM. Serenity. A transcendental oneness with the universe. You should be taking comfort in the phrase of the great Englishman, John Maynard Keynes, economist, humanist, pederast: 'In the long run we are all dead.' "

The sound and camera crew rescued Alec. They posed him under the metal flagpoles, and he earnestly spoke of the World Body, its mysteries, and the hope it engendered in every visitor. They taped twenty minutes and expected to use five.

That evening, Alec settled himself before his little set and watched the 6:30 news.

Dean Steed, the anchorman, opened with invasions and incursions. On-location footage followed from Algeria and Paris, trailed by some hastily edited and blurry images from the Middle East. There was nothing from the WEB. At 6:18, immediately after a commercial for a decongestant,

Crow came on with Eddie Sale, a baseball manager whose team had finished in the cellar the year before. "We're gonna surprise a lot of people," he said. "It's a long season, and in 162 games intangibles come to the surface. This team comes to play. They give 110 percent."

He was followed by a woman with large isobars explaining why the weather was unseasonable, and a man with a pushbroom mustache who reviewed a movie about a model married to an orangutan.

Alec spent the next morning alternately attending plenary sessions and hysterical meetings and calling the network. He was not able to reach Grambling until late afternoon.

"Why didn't you use my stuff?" Alec demanded.

"We're saving it for a special." Grambling was abstracted. "Keep up the work. The General likes it. Wants to see you sometime soon."

"When?"

"Soon. Keep digging."

"For what?"

"How the hell do I know for what? Why didn't you get the story on that greaser?" he countered, and hung up.

"What story?" Alec asked into the dead phone. He shuffled the newspaper. The story sat smugly on page five under Hackett's byline: "The government of El Chazade is now in the hands of the freely elected representatives of the Guardia Royale, a group of nine colonels of the army and air force. Former President Juan Garcia-Krauss is under house arrest in the capital city, pending trial for crimes against the state . . ."

Hackett, full of unusually good spirits, took Alec to the delegates' gym, where he had guest privileges. In an area larger than half a football field, men went through contortions similar to those recorded by Dante. A turbaned Indian jogged furiously on a treadmill, like a man in a dream. Two Sikhs threw a medicine ball at each other's stomachs with mechanical ferocity. A group of Englishmen did squat knee thrusts in time to a greatly amplified version of "Short People." An Israeli played Ping-Pong with a Spaniard who went back from the table twenty and thirty feet to return the ball, screaming *"Andare!"* with every stroke.

"Back ye lily-livered scum!" bellowed a simian instructor to a group of Sikhs miserably doing pushups. "Avast ye scuppers—" He turned away and in a loud voice greeted Hackett: "Hello Bill! New boy?"

Hackett introduced his charge. "Alec Lessing, Rafe Powers."

"Delighted!" said Rafe. He smiled, turned away, and began screaming, "Awright, scum, gimme ten!" in the voice of a boatswain.

"Tough man, that," said Hackett. "Had a very good war."

"Looks familiar," Alec commented.

"Ought to. Served with all the giants: Robert Taylor, Van Johnson, Duke Wayne. Five years at MGM. Kept up morale. Got a medal from MacArthur. Best as a pirate, though. All the critics said so. Help yourself, Squire."

Hackett wandered off and sat in a rowing machine. Alec took the one beside him. Both men began to row. Within two minutes, Hackett, red-faced and puffing, slowed to an indolent rhythm reminiscent of a man trolling for bass. Nearby a squat Oriental built on the order of a fireplug yelled imprecations at a smaller black man with pronounced tribal scars on his cheeks.

"That's Han Weng," said Hackett.

"Chinese?"

"He'd like you to think so."

"Pretty bad mood he's in."

"Weng's always like that to blacks. He hates racism. And Africans still trade with the West."

Alec started to protest. Hackett dismissed him. "Can't argue with success, Squire." He shrugged and went back to rowing.

But that was all I used to do, Alec thought. At Princeton he had wrangled with extinct powers: kings and poet laureates. As a critic he was always taking issue with long-running hits. Even in Europe he would occasionally challenge ministers and barons. But in New York, at the WEB, everything was slippery and undersized, more foreign than Sanskrit, more remote than the Orinoco. There must be a way into this society, he reasoned. They couldn't all be buffoons. Otherwise the world was on its way to lava and dust.

There seemed no way to glean anything from the invisible press corps, or from Hackett, or from anyone at the network. A name peeked briefly out from his brain, like an animal, and then withdrew. He waited for it to emerge again. The name advanced tentatively from its burrow and Alec pounced. Ellenbogen. The previous WEB correspondent. Now writing a book somewhere.

Network personnel had a forwarding address on Canal Street but the telephone number was unlisted. Alec went downtown, walked around the building, certain that he had been misdirected. The warehouse was four stories high and in a state of despair. The last tenant had been Rob Roy Finials, wholesale only, but it had obviously vacated the premises long ago. The windows were painted over and a chain fence drawn across them. Alec tried the rusty door. It opened onto a small, dirty hallway. The tile floor was besmeared and dotted with L-shaped cigarette butts. It smelled of Lysol, roach spray, and indefinable decay. He lit a match to illuminate three doorbells and the nameplates beside them. One was unmarked, another said Rob Roy Deliveries in Back. The third read Reece-Ellenbogen. Alec pushed it.

A great clattering of ungreased machinery began. At his back Alec saw the limp guide wires of a freight elevator as it sank with a discouraging moan to the main floor. Its narrow accordion gate remained closed. A round homunculus, neatly bearded and dressed in a Savile Row suit, peered out.

"You are?"

"Alec Lessing."

"What do you want?"

The gate swung open when Alec told him.

Gregory Ellenbogen extended a soft hand. "Ah. Well. So. They found a replacement. At long last. Step in. Forgive the background. Necessary for anonymity."

It was only when Alec entered that he noticed the sword-faced man in fatigues, with bandolier slung across his chest and grenades dangling from his belt.

"This is Heitor," Ellenbogen said. "I once did a trifling favor for his family when they wanted to leave Cuba. He and his brothers were all to be shot. Somehow they escaped. Since then he's been in my service. An excellent driver, of all my cars. But he handles the Mercedes best. Even better than the Bentley, I think." Heitor ran the elevator to the top floor. They stepped out into a garden. A rose trellis held a hundred blossoms, and irises and dahlias implausibly bloomed under the klieg lights. The aroma, aided by incense, was stifling. Something brayed in the background. Nearby, black goats chewed envelopes from a wicker basket. Marble fountains plashed and small trees shone in the tinted sunlight, filtered through erotic stained-glass panels in the ceiling. In a long, shallow pond frogs capered on lilypads, snapping occasionally at tiger

swallowtail butterflies. Sharp silvery fish swam by and disappeared in plastic reeds.

"Pike and pickerel," said Ellenbogen. "Strictly for my
guests. Those who are amused to fish for their lunch. They
tell me the meat is very sweet and translucent. Personally,
I'm allergic. Something to drink?"

He indicated a narrow polished table of malachite and
inlaid garnet. A silver wine bucket held three uncorked
bottles of Chardonnay from an unknown vineyard. "My
own label. A hobby." Ellenbogen poured two glasses.
"Now," he asked Alec as they sat down, "give me the details."

Alec told him of the vanished or alcoholic press corps,
of the undersized simultaneous translator who slept in containers, and the indifference of the staff to worldwide chaos
and war, of the diffidence at the network. "I don't understand it," he said finally. "The General himself put me
here, but I can't get on the air."

Gregory Ellenbogen listened with his eyes shut and
his fingertips touching. As Alec spoke he felt an enclosure
around his words, like a balloon around the speech of people in a comic strip. Ellenbogen was a parvenu with various
sensual delights at hand, a vinyl caliph. Possessor of an
independent income. What did he care about the WEB
now? Probably he had taken the job of correspondent as a
lark, a chance to meet a new international set. A dollar-a-
year man. Alec was sorry now that he had come at all.

At length Ellenbogen said, "I can't help you. Really.
I thought you knew about the WEB. It's like Las Vegas: a
serious joke. Attracts the lowest and the highest. Every
government has a representative. But the only reason they
come is to get away from home: DPL plates and parties
at the embassy. Kings have appeared there, and oil sheiks
and presidents. Because of the captive audience. And

what an audience: The young are ignorant, the elder states-
men are senile. And the press! With certain exceptions, of
course."

"Like you."

"No, I was as bad as the rest. Only while they were
drinking and whoring I was—well, all I can tell you is that
five years ago I was writing press releases for the WEB.
You know: 'But it isn't all work. Here we see some
Ecuadorian delegates dancing away the concerns of state.'
Then I got a job at the network. They needed a WEB
correspondent. At five-fifty a week, plus expenses. Not bad.
But I only got one raise in three years."

Alec looked around the room. "That must have been
some raise."

"Not really." Ellenbogen smiled wanly and got to his
feet. "I guess I haven't been of much help. But of course
there're some things one simply can't talk about."

He saw Alec out. The Cuban ran ahead and unbolted
the many locks and bowed as Ellenbogen and Alec passed
by. Alec joined another Cuban in the elevator. This time
the host stayed outside and looked in. The Cuban closed the
accordion gate. "There's still plenty of it lying around,"
Ellenbogen shouted as the elevator started down. "For a
clever man, I mean."

It was raining when Alec reached the street. Fine
spray slicked the asphalt and darkened the sides of buildings. The colors of the afternoon were at the somber end
of the spectrum, an antidote to the glitter upstairs. What
Ellenbogen's zircon manner signified Alec could not guess.
A hick's idea of elegance, maybe. A pimp's notion of the
good life. Even so, it cost money to live that way. A flow
of cash or services. *There's still plenty of it lying around. For
a clever man, I mean.* What could the WEB produce in the
way of income, even for a hyena journalist? Blackmail?
Drugs? Procuring? Anything like that could be a terrific

exposé. Award stuff. An international Watergate.

Near Hudson Street a television store displayed an array of sets, tuned to different stations. All were broadcasting the early evening news, even the channels that normally reran "M*A*S*H" and "The Odd Couple." An Argentinian was crying angry tears on one. Bombs exploded in Antwerp on another.

Alec spent the weekend fixing up his new place. He bought a door, laid it sideways across the small bookshelves, and turned it into a desk. He filled the shelves with the volumes from his father's house, augmented with a bagful of paperbacks and remainders he bought at a bookstore on upper Broadway. He stocked the refrigerator with milk and Guinness and white wine and eleven chocolate bars and a box of marzipan rolled in balls and tinted to the color of oranges and apples and cherries. Then he called his daughter and asked her to spend the day with him at the museum.

She met him outside her building, to avoid a confrontation with Laura. They rode the bus in silence. Around them passengers' voices boomed like radios, speculating about the news. Azie did not respond to Alec's questions and they continued in silence, reading their books. Azie was deep in Aesop; her father read *The Hedgehog and the Fox*. At Fifty-seventh Street Azie examined the jacket of Alec's book. "Want to trade?" she offered. Alec handed his volume over and accepted the *Fables* in exchange.

"This isn't about animals." She sounded cruelly deceived.

"It's about people who are *like* animals," her father said. "Some people are like foxes; they know a lot of little things. Other people are like hedgehogs. They know one big thing."

"Like Mom is a hedgehog."

"I would have thought a fox."

"No, you're a fox. You know a lot of stuff. You're always talking about different things. On television, I mean."

"But I know one big thing. I knew when I went overseas I would come back and be with you."

"That's a little thing."

"Not to me." He returned her book. "What does Mom know?"

"I don't know. But it's too big for her."

Alec stopped prodding when they reached the museum. The place was unusually empty, except for groups of Japanese tourists laden with cameras, and some sullen schoolchildren towed by the will of their *au pair* girls.

The place had lost none of its power; he had spent much of his childhood in these wide corridors, away from the Wizard's clamorous magic. It was free in those days and he would be there when the museum opened and stay inside, nibbling his swiss cheese sandwich, wandering through the African veldt and the Indian plains, vanishing into the dioramas, intimate of elephant, deer, and Blackfoot, until the 5:00 bell reminded him to go home.

Alec and Azie stopped to contemplate the drama of a tiger pouncing on a gazelle. A voice beside them said: "This is the way I imagine heaven to be."

It was Pandit the translator. Alec introduced him. Azie listened, absorbed, as the little man gesticulated violently.

"Everything frozen in time. This is what it must be like in paradise. The fruit is hanging heavy, but never quite ripe enough to fall off. Oh no! And the tiger leaping, but never quite catching its terrified victim. Like one's self and a woman: in sight, touchable, able to be caressed, palpated, erotic, yet at the same time beyond reach. Your first time?"

Azie shook her head vigorously. "I come here all the time."

"Tell me, which is your favorite?"

"Well, I—"

"My own is the insects. Six legs. I adore immoderately legs."

"The masks, I guess. I especially like the one that's a mask and when you open it there's another mask inside."

"Amazing! I have not seen it. I must go." He offered a thin, bony hand to father and daughter and retreated, still facing them, like a courtier, bowing slightly, withdrawing from the royal presence. "Who has done this mask?" he shouted at the end of the hall.

"Indians," said Azie.

"American Indians. Not Indian Indians."

"Yes."

"I thought as much. Primitive art is the most sophisticated. Puzzling, yet at the same time clear. A mask inside a mask. It could be a parable of the WEB! Good-bye." And he was gone.

Azie watched the place where Pandit had been. A fox, she decided.

When Alec came in to work the next day he received the first bit of good news since his return to New York. Ambassador Steelhead, the United States Representative to the World Body, would see him. The appointment was for 3:00.

Alec went to the network library and took down two folders of clips on Steelhead. The first offered little more than the skeletal components of biography. Lance Xavier Steelhead, son of an Iranian-Irish mother and an American

Indian father, hence Steelhead, a fish found near the ancestral waters of the Nisqually in Washington State. A rapid rise from a Seattle public school to an athletic scholarship in hockey to Dartmouth; from there to Harvard Law, Chief Justice Bland's law clerk, prosecutor for the federal government, private practice, an unsuccessful attempt to run for office in the Silk Stocking district of Manhattan, more private practice, a career as defense attorney for unpopular causes: usurers, axe murderers, child molesters, Nazis, pyromaniacs, sadists, kidnappers, terrorists; all the while moving around Manhattan, seeking a safe seat until, at last, he found one on the West Side, ran for Congress, and squeaked in. In the hall of the House of Representatives his speeches were considered, as the president later said, "so memorable that we thought they deserved a different, larger forum." The second folder, somewhat larger, concerned Steelhead's career at the WEB. "Ambassador says U.S. Plans Invasion of Paraguay," one headline read. This was followed by another entry from a later headline: "Steelhead consults president, says, 'I misspoke myself' on Paraguay invasion, meant evasion." Another read: "Ambassador asks Elizabeth II to step down." In later stories "down" was changed to "aside." Then "lively" and finally "in."

Similar clippings told of other controversies. The ambassador saw himself as St. Sebastian, riddled with arrows from special interest groups. After a whirlwind tour of the Middle East, he pronounced the sheikdoms "democracies in embryo, lacking only *habeas corpus*, women's suffrage, and running water to make them the equal of any Western society." He called the white race the cancer of history, and then modified it to pneumonia and, ultimately, sniffles. Wherever he spoke he kicked up the dust of academia; professors denounced him for calling Confucius a fascist, or Mount Rushmore part of the military industrial complex. Still he persisted, still he spoke. Congressmen called for his resignation; foreign governments complained to the White House. Yet Ambassador Steelhead remained, as secure and surly as a traffic court judge. In general he stayed away from the press; he had once called them "shmucks with Underwoods" and they never forgave him. But now and then, depending on whim and how much pressure had been placed upon him in Washington, he allowed a journalist in his office. Evidently the urging had been great; Alec had to wait less than two hours before he was ushered into the ambassadorial quarters.

Steelhead sat watching television on a small screen. Upon Alec's entrance he rose, shook hands, and sank again into his chair. The rerun blared on. Steelhead gave no further acknowledgment of his guest's existence. Instead, he bellowed merrily at each sight gag and punch line. When the program ended he switched the set off and turned to Alec. His eyes were still wet from laughter.

"That Gomer Pyle," he said when he recovered his wind. "The power struggle between authority and the seemingly deprived but eventually victorious underlings. Almost a poem of colonial oppression, with the formerly enslaved throwing off the yoke of oppression. But, to be serious for a moment . . ." He scrutinized his guest. "Why are you here?"

"You invited me. I got a call."

"Ah. Lessing. From the network. Yes. Coffee?"

"No thank you."

That seemed to end the interview. Nothing was said. The clock printed out its digits; steam rose from the official mug embossed with eagle and crossed spears. Steelhead seemed to be weighing some alternatives. He held up four fingers. "You're here for three reasons." He looked at his hand and withdrew a digit. "One, you're new and I grant every World Body correspondent an interview. Two, frankly, I need network exposure now. To get across the

United States's position," he added hastily. "We're speaking off the record. And three, your predecessor left here very rapidly. Too rapidly. I thought perhaps you knew why."

"I was in Europe when he left."

"Ah. But you did know Mr. Ellenbogen?"

"Only on TV."

"A pig. Always rooting around for scandal. He told me he was onto something. When I reminded him of this later, he said that he was drunk. What happened to him?"

"He's in the private sector," said Alec, slipping into the jargon.

"Where he belongs. Now, tell me, what are you on the lookout for?"

"War." Alec showily put away his notebook to assure the ambassador of privacy. "How close are we to the real thing?"

"On the bad side, it looks dire. On the good side, it always looks dire."

Their conversation was interrupted by sounds of shouts and scufflings in the corridor. The two men rose, but before they could get to the door it was flung open and one of the WEB guards ran in.

"Stay inside!" he shouted. "Get down! Hide!"

Alec was too curious to duck and Steelhead stubbornly refused to move. "What the hell is going on here?" He looked for the guard. "Where are you?"

"Somebody fired shots," came a muffled voice from the closet. "Hide! How can I protect you if you won't hide?"

Steelhead strode to the door and peered down the hallway. A group of delegates was talking with great agitation. A medical team knelt beside a body. Alec and Steelhead approached them. Pandit appeared.

"Oh, my goodness," said the translator. "I should have stayed home this day. It is distinctly a bad day. The anniversary of my wedding. Festive, yet at the same time tragic. Poor man." He regarded the supine figure. Alec began to reconstruct the scenario; off to the side stood the emir, shaking his head. Near him was the reliable Daladan, carefully explaining to a listener. Alec showed his press pass and advanced on the emir.

"They shall pay dearly for this," the potentate vowed. "Do they think I am made of chauffeurs? Do they think chauffeurs grow on trees? Human rights indeed! What about the human rights of absolute monarchs? Have emirs no feelings? We also need food and oil. Where is the new leadership to come from?" he asked Alec. "From the camel drivers? The agitators?"

Daladan subtly interposed himself between the royal presence and the interviewer. "An absurd mistake has been made," he insisted. "A dastardly attempt on the life of the emir, who only desires peace and a democratic secular state. America is a country of gangsters and thugs, toward which we bear no ill will." He and a phalanx of bodyguards accompanied the emir, still protesting, down the corridor, away from foreign journalists. Alec had started back to the ambassador's office when he saw the Lilliputian. He stood at the far end of the hall, a diminutive, shadowy figure with a pair of opera glasses, examining the fallen man. He shook his head.

"Did you see that?" Alec asked Steelhead.

"See what?"

"The man. The little man at the end of the hall."

"Escudero? The Mad Mosquito? Why?"

"You said his name was?"

"Angel Escudero. A Central American delegate. Excuse me." Distressed, Steelhead scratched his head. "I'll have to make calls. Unprecedented. Terrible."

"Of course," Alec said, and sped downstairs.

He took a cab to the network. This time he would not

allow Grambling to put him off. There was the stuff of headlines here, evidence of betrayal and intrigue and revelation. Even the high-speed elevator seemed to drag as it shot him up to the executive suite. Below, on the working areas, the forty-seventh floor was referred to as Krypton, a place where life, as we know it, is said to exist. Few employees had been allowed here, where prime ministers and heavyweight champions had been kept waiting, where elections had been determined, and international reputations made and ruined. But that did not deter Alec; he had fire in his eye and news to report.

He ran to Grambling's office, past secretaries and waiting technicians. Grambling was on the telephone. "Right away, General," he was saying, as Alec appeared in the doorway. A buzzer sounded. "Yes!" Grambling yelled into a phone. "All right, put him on. Yes, Senator. I know about it. We're very, very sorry. The retraction goes on the air at 7:10. Yes sir, thank you." He picked up another phone and ordered: "Get this out now, tonight on the 7:00 news: 'The network deeply regrets the computer error last night about Representative Bland. A retraction will be read tonight at 7:10 before the break.' Period. That's all. Jesus." Grambling turned to look at Alec, but his face betrayed no recognition. He seemed to be talking to his desk. "You'd think that capon would know a misprint, but no. It says so on the teleprompter, he reads it: 'Representative Miles Bland smilingly received an award from the B'nai B'rith as New York's friendliest gay.' His fiancée broke their engagement, his mother won't talk to him; the General chewed my ass five times this afternoon. We were supposed to say *goy*. Oh, Christ." The glaze between the speaker and audience vanished and Grambling barked: "What do *you* want? By God, it better be good."

Alec told him about the Lilliputian in the airplane, about the attempts on the emir's life, about Ellenbogen under constant private guard, about the ominous sense of things at the WEB, about the shooting in the hall while he and Steelhead talked. Grambling looked at him, stunned. "Is *that* all?" he asked.

"'Is *that* all?'" Laura asked. "That's what he said? Honestly?"

Alec was returning Azie. He had hoped not to run into Laura, but there she was, unavoidable, at the door. When she asked how things were going, Alec told her. "He said lintheads were out of season. All he wants is Russia versus China, Africa versus Africa, or U.S. versus everybody."

"The rest goes down the toilet." Azie had heard the story earlier, on the bus.

"The rest of what goes down the toilet?" A man's voice echoed from the kitchen. Laura opened the door all the way and brought on her bullet-headed friend. He had an open shirt and a quantity of body hair. He wore a silver scarab medallion on a silver chain; a copper bracelet decorated his right wrist and braided elephant hair circled his left. His boots were by Frye and his jeans by Jordache and he paced with an urgent gait, like a man in search of a drugstore. He was introduced as Reed Lupien, co-owner of Lupien and Cross, Publishers, Los Angeles.

"We're into herbs and children," Alec was informed.

"You going to publish Laura's work?"

"I don't know. I just flashed on it. It looks like our kind of material. We need stuff that gets kids in touch with their karma. Gemini, sort of. Like Laura." He gave her arm a small squeeze. At other times, Alec and Laura would have exchanged a private look and done something with their eyebrows. But he did not dare to look at her now.

Reed turned to him: "What's your sign?"

"Deer crossing." This was met with silence, so Alec relented: "Taurus."

"There's your trouble. Taurus doesn't mix with anything except Sagittarius. Didn't you know?"

"I've been in Europe."

"Yeah, well. So. Whaddya think of the way Laura's getting her shit together?"

"Unbelievable."

"Me too. You wanna stay for dinner? Beans and rice."

"No, I—"

"Got all the amino acids."

"I have a dinner date," Alec lied, and kissed Azie goodbye and shook hands with Reed, and then with Laura.

He went directly from the apartment to a singles bar and picked up the first woman without two heads. They drank more than they ate, and went to her place, although it was only five blocks from Alec's, because he wanted to wake up alone; he had always wanted to wake up alone, he thought, as he followed her up the stairs. No voices in the morning, coloring the day before its form had been decided. Same old Alec.

Her name was Tina Jean and she was not one of the sad ones, which was a blessing; there were pictures of a number of men pinned to her bulletin board. She had only one kink. She liked to make love with all the lights on and every appliance plugged in and going: the VCR, the stereo, the vacuum cleaner, the Cuisinart, the electric typewriter, the electric pencil sharpener, the microwave oven, the sunlamp.

"Plug me!" her contralto sounded over the noise. "You're a new appliance and I'm a wall socket."

"What?" Alec shouted. "I can't hear you. The vacuum cleaner."

"I said—never mind."

"What?"

"Just *plug* me!"

He plugged. Despite her idiosyncrasy, Alec later decided, she was ordinary household current. Which was just as well.

He made his way back to the new apartment during the small rush hour, sharing the subway car with cleaning ladies. Several glared at him, as if they had heard that this was the man who threw humans away in wastebaskets. He snored on the IRT, went past his stop, and arrived home too fatigued to change into pajamas. He fell asleep on top of the bedspread and did not awaken until he heard the rataplan of soldiers drilling on the street below.

3

He had forgotten. It was Armed Forces Day. Down the Drive they came, pennants swirling, flags snapping in the off-river gusts, the army, navy, coast guard, marines and sanitation department. A vast and fluid crowd cheered along the sidewalks, back of the gray wooden barriers. Assortments of psychopaths sporadically interrupted with gestures of overappreciation or contempt, but their cries were lost in the wind. Each militiaman moved with eyes front, imperturbable, staring at the neck of the marcher before him. Behind each battalion wheeled exhibits of nuclear missiles and neutron bombs, gentled down the street as if they were floats in the Rose Bowl.

From his window Alec could see a parade-stand four blocks away. He found his binoculars, swept the crowd and the stand itself. The mayor was there, head gleaming cheerily in the early sun. Some other unidentifiable dignitaries in dark coats flanked him. Off to the side, another shaved dome attracted Alec's attention. He washed and shaved hurriedly and bloodily, threw on his clothes, wrapped himself in a trench coat, and went outside.

It was difficult to make his way down to the stand, but by moving with eccentric thrusts he managed to arrive just as the General's final bromides were amplified by a distorting loudspeaker. A Secret Service man moved in as Alec approached, but General Wolfe waved him away. "Lessing, isn't it? I thought so," he said.

"Yes," Alec replied.

"What did you think of the parade? An absolute knockout."

"Magnificent. General, I've been trying to reach you all week—"

Wolfe started off for his limousine.

"About what?"

"The World Body."

"The WEB?"

"Yes."

"This way."

Once in the car, without pausing for breath, Alec again unreeled the events of the past week, with particular emphasis on the Lilliputian. He sidestepped Grambling's sourness, and he left out Ellenbogen entirely. He did not finish until they were at the network.

Halfway out of the car, the General ordered: "Go down to the WEB and start to work on that little man. Obviously sugar-crazed. All reports direct to me: Eyes Only. Now, this is absolutely key: Ambassador Steelhead. You've met him? I thought so."

"Once."

"Watch him. Very, *very* closely. An extremely dangerous type. About your stuff getting on the news: We'll have it on soon enough. A word to the wise." And he was gone.

Alec scribbled notes on the back of a pay envelope as the car took him crosstown. But when he got to his office an unexpected presence bothered his thoughts and work. A group of foreign dignitaries and some pressmen circled his desk, where a man, blocked from view, was gesticulating.

"Pop!"

"Alec! I dropped by to give you the wonderful news!

I'm going to be a father. Select three cards. Any three."

Resistance was hopeless. Alec played the shill; he took three cards and put them back in the deck. They vanished in a shuffle; two later surfaced, one under the seat of a Burmese delegate, the other in the wallet of a man from the *Times*. The response was aboriginal. Eyes widened, cheers resounded. Someone passed around a bottle of Scotch before the witnesses scattered, shaking their heads, leaving father and son alone.

"Do you have to put on a show every time you go anywhere?" Alec demanded. "The world is falling apart and all you can do is sleight of hand."

"Alec, Alec." The old man put his arm around his son's shoulder. "We're in the same business. Illusion." He produced the third card from his son's ear.

Alec opened his mouth to protest, then closed it. He reddened. "*Now* who did you get pregnant?"

"Your mother. A menopause baby."

"She's sixty-three years old, Pop. She went through a change of life years ago."

"Apparently not. Read this."

He handed Alec a postcard. "I am with child," it read. "Returning home shortly. Naming it Anthony, after Susan B."

"That doesn't mean she's pregnant." Alec steamed around the room. "She's just with *a* child. Probably adopted some native. Jesus, all I need is a little brother named Susan B. Anthony."

The Wizard stared at the postcard with an air of resignation. "A pity," he said. "I would have been a good father."

"Second time around, maybe."

The telephone rang. It was for the Wizard. The conversation was monosyllabic. Josiah Lessing revived as he hung up. "Two more club dates in Atlantic City. Until then I was wondering if, perhaps . . ."

"How much?"

"A century?"

Alec wrote a check for a hundred dollars. Better the old man than Hackett.

"A peculiar thing, Alec; a paradox. The poor, who need money the most, are the very ones who never have it. God bless. Would you like to see a coin trick?"

"No."

The Wizard did the Dime that ate New York, the Shrinking Hat, and the Farting Dollar. Then, mercifully, he disappeared, clinking his change down the hallway. Alec waited until the sound of silver had evaporated. Then with slow, deliberate, supremely rational movements he dialed the number he had unobtrusively spotted on Ellenbogen's phone.

It rang a long time before a heavily accented voice answered.

"Who ees talkeen?" He pronounced the *l* in talking.

"This is Alec Lessing. Mr. Ellenbogen will speak to me if you tell him who it is."

There was an inaudible negotiation followed by humming. In a minute the voice came on. "He will see jou thees offernoon at 3:00."

"I want to talk to him now."

"Jou will be here at 3:00."

"I will be there at 3:00."

Alec put down the receiver and thought about calling Steelhead, but a voice interrupted him.

"Pardon."

It belonged to a man with a turban and a Western suit. Something glittered in his eyes. Tears, maybe, or avarice. It reminded Alec of his father's stage expression: move a little closer, yokels. "Would you excuse me for a minute?" he said, and without waiting for an answer got out of the room, the building, and the neighborhood.

What Alec wanted most of all was to talk to a woman. In the old days he used to sit on the floor and speak to Laura. That was impossible now, and there was no one in all of Manhattan to whom he could turn. Those he had left behind in Europe were scarcely recollected now; there *was* one, Yvette, a student, who was a great listener, who loved, after bed, to sit and smoke and quote Stendhal on love. She spoke English with a comic accent; she called it "fokine," like the choreographer: "I don't fill like fokine just yet, let's go to the cinema." But she had married a wine merchant and gone to live in Alsace. He wondered briefly what it would cost to call Yvette and what time it was in Alsace. But he had forgotten her new name.

He walked through the city, occasionally shoved by crowds on the sidewalk or tyrannized by drivers at street corners making lefts into his path. The leer of the gutter and the heavy smell of burning oil and burned falafel were all around him; he walked on, numb. He wound up at Laura's and pressed the buzzer. There was no answer. Alec went to the corner and hesitated for a long time before he called Rose at work.

"Hello."

"Alec?"

"Yes."

"God!"

"Dinner?"

"No."

"Drink?"

"No!"

"Please?"

"*Al*ec—"

"Yes?"

"No."
"Why?"
"Because."
"Lunch?"
"I—"
"Yes?"
"When?"
"Now."
"Where?"
"Palmetto."

Rose, on whom he had spent all that time, the beloved he had fought and mollified and apologized to and yelled at; whose marriage had bent and buckled because of him, but never ended, as his own did; sentimental Rose, whose eyes filled up at Bufferin commercials, who swore that once he went to Europe she would never see him again, would switch off the set if he ever appeared on it, burn his letters and the picture Crow had taken of them: Rose, just like that, consented to see him.

Warmth radiated southward from his heart. One thing about Rose, he thought: she was preeminently sane. Even in the throes of love, on the worst stolen afternoons at the hotel, the two of them commiserating about the aches of these adulterous interludes, she never lost control as he did. Always there would come a silence, a grace note. The sun's angle, maybe, or a quick glance at her watch, or some internal mechanism. "It's time," she would say, and put her hand on the back of his neck in the funny way she had. And sometimes they would make love again, and sometimes they would dress silently. Either way there was a melancholy undertow to those two words. A sense of something programmed in its genes to be incomplete, a dwarf affair.

And yet there she was, sitting at a table in the back. Smart lady; the reservation had already been made in his name. She had touched her cheekbones with a bit of color;

she always knew to the grain how much kohl to use on her eyes. The blonde hair caught the light; she looked smashing and, as before, she knew it. A big dazzle from the mouth, and a display of the fine neck. "Hello, Alec," was all she said.

He sat down and looked at her. He was staring, he realized, and looked away. The waitress brought him a glass of white wine.

"I took the liberty," Rose explained. "You haven't changed, have you?"

"In any way."

"Same old Alec."

"So everyone tells me."

"Tell me. About everything. Europe, Azie. Everything."

And he did. It took them through the omelet and the salad and two more drinks. Rose was particularly interested in Azie, but the next favorite character in Alec's summary was Ellenbogen. The notion of goats and butterflies in a loft appealed to her. Especially goats. Every time Alec started talking about assassins or war, Rose switched the subject to goats.

"Rose," he insisted, "this is not a farce."

"Of course it is. That's what makes it serious."

He thought about that over dessert. "I don't know what to do." Alec kept staring at her.

"Go back to your old job. I always thought you were a good teacher."

"Yes. Well. Teach."

He tried not to look at her breasts.

"Don't get hooked," she said.

"It was always easy for me to get hooked, Rose."

"On the WEB, I mean." She gave him a sidelong, corrective glance. "And please, please stop looking at me like that."

"Like what?"

"As if I was the pronoun and you were the verb."

"I am the verb."

Out on the street, Rose said suddenly, "Alec. I can't."

He nodded. "I didn't ask."

"Only with your eyes."

But when he kissed her goodbye it was her eyes that were wet. He stayed too long on her mouth and then in it. She always tasted of the sea.

"Rose. Take the afternoon off," he said.

"I can't. And neither can you. You have an appointment with Ellenbogen in ten minutes."

"The hell with Ellenbogen. I'll see him tomorrow."

Nuns went by.

"I must be crazy," she said after a while. Buses migrated north; cabs clanged over manholes. At the Plaza she said it again. "I wanted you dead," she confessed.

"Me too."

"Wanted me dead, or you?"

"Me. You. It. I was crazy then."

"And this is sane?"

"Why not?"

"Well. I'm still married to Mel. I'll always be married to Mel."

"I know."

"Only now you don't care."

"I care. I just don't mind."

"What's that supposed to mean?"

He gave no answer; he had none. Except that while he looked at the topography of her body, now lying across the brown satin quilt, he kept thinking of his ex-wife and her San Francisco animal.

"What time is it?" Rose asked.

He ransacked the rapidly discarded clothes for his watch. "Four-twenty."

"God! Let me call my office."

"Truth is the best lie."

"Mimi? I didn't have anybody coming up this after-noon did I? God! It completely slipped my . . . God! Tell him to wait, will you, Meem? I'll be there in ten."

Rose sat up and held her head in her hands. She looked at Alec. "I forgot my goddam anniversary. Mel's on his way over. God! And women are supposed to be the sentimental ones."

She raised her voice and began a litany of their mis-timed adventures, ranging back over three years. To drown out the highs, Alec switched on the hotel TV set. The Mad Mosquito appeared in a crowd. The image twisted and righted itself. Alec turned up the sound. "Ellenbogen," said the voice, and Rose quieted. The screen showed red flames. Rose came and sat by Alec. She felt warm. Her bones were thin. He put his hand on her knee, but now without signifi-cance, and heard the voice talk about a Canal Street fire, and about the man who lived on the top floor where the catastrophe occurred. A fire inspector at the scene testified that no one could have got out alive. A gas explosion, he thought.

Alec and Rose watched as the front of the building collapsed. The bricks fell like water, pounding into the street. Smoke and dust covered them.

"Poor goats," was all she said.

At the WEB he tried to locate Steelhead, but the am-bassador had gone on a mission to Washington. Alec toyed briefly with the idea of befriending, possibly even romanc-ing, the ambassador's secretary. But he could not find her. The legend *Dale Knowles* was on a wooden marker atop her desk. He noted the name, tried to fit a face to it, recalled nothing, and, after a guard had gone by, surreptitiously examined a wastebasket. It was full of excelsior. Of course, he thought, the ambassador, like everyone on the staff, would have a shredder. Alec would have to try something else.

On the way to his office he stopped by at the press room. Hackett was there, making neat piles of ten-dollar bills.

He looked up when Alec came in.

"Hello, Squire," he said pleasantly. "Heard about Ellenbogen?"

"Yes. I just saw it on TV."

"Bad show. Strange man. Corrupt, indecent, a real sneak thief. Yet, despite all that, a really *aw*ful chap. Did you know him?"

"We met. I see you got paid."

"This? Poker game last night." The information was followed by a galvanic wink. "That's how it's done, Squire."

"How what's done?"

"The payoffs. Nobody slips you money under the table anymore. You sort of win it at cards. If the IRS ever examines your bank account, you tell them you got lucky is all."

Alec thought about this odd reversal of tradition. "You mean, they arrange the game so you win?"

"Now you're catching on, Squire."

"Who is they?"

"Depends on the goods and services rendered. Did I mention there's a fellow waiting at your desk? A linthead."

Alec suddenly recalled the man from hours before, with the wild gaze. Before further inquiries could be made, Hackett went off to spend his new money. Reluctantly, Alec returned to his desk. The man looked precisely the same, as if he had been posing for a sculptor since the last meeting.

"Ah! Welcome back!" he shouted.

Alec regarded him warily. "Have you been here all this time?"

"Maurice Damar, Morocco." The little man bowed. "I have been waiting forevre, it seems."

"I'm sorry. There were things—"

"Nothing. It was worth. Your fathre, he ees the Wizaird, not?"

"That's what he calls himself."

"I admair very much the man that he perform alone. By 'imself. I would like to have an introduction."

"Fine. Leave your name and address."

"I also want to perform."

"Fine. He—"

"Not for me, of course, the trick. I want to get yauks."

"Yauks?"

"Oui. Yes. Yauks. Boffeaux. Bellai laughs. 'Enny Youngman, Zhoie Bishoppe, Sheky Grin. All Zionists. I will be the first Arab stands-up comedianne. What do you think of these:

"Good evening ladies and germs." The Moroccan put his thumbs behind his lapels and struck the attitude of a Las Vegas emcee. "It sims a man had a parrot. But 'e 'ad to go out of town for a wik. So 'e give the parrot to 'is mothair. When 'e gets back 'e says to maman, 'Ow was the bird?' The mothair, she replies, saying, 'It was delicieuse.' 'What!' says the man. 'Mothair, that was a very valuable bird. It spauk seven languages.' 'Well then,' says maman, 'why didn't 'e say something?' "

He waited for Alec's response. Alec forced a smile. The Moroccan continued:

"I pass Four Saisons restaurant. A pan'andler, 'e stop me. 'Pardon,' 'e says. ''Ave you got 150 dollars and 25 cents for a cup of coffee?' I tell 'im, 'Coffee's only a quartière.' 'E says, 'You don't expect me to go in zere dressed like these, do you?' "

During the routine, Alec drummed his fingers on the desktop, looked around, and thought about wandering away. But as Maurice Damar finished, an idea came.

"I'll give you my father's phone number and address, if you do me one small favor," he offered.

"Anytheeng."

"You know Angel Escudero?"

"The Mad Mosquito? We 'ave met at embassy parties."

"I want to meet him."

"'E is a very shy man. 'Ates meeting with journalistes."

"Well, my father hates meetings with amateurs."

"I see."

Damar walked around, deciding.

"I do it," he announced. "I want very bad to get boffeaux."

"Yocks."

"Yes."

Two days later the Wizard telephoned to complain about the Arab comic:

"Bore."

"Agreed."

"Maniac."

"Probably."

"Necessary?"

"Vital."

"Right."

"Thanks."

An hour after, the Lilliputian called. "The Moroccan has spoken to me. I will see you. You talk my language?"

"No," Alec admitted. "Shall I bring an interpreter?"

"I will bring. You be at Disco 33⅓ now."

The place was already filled and loud. The Lilliputian sat at a table accompanied by an even smaller citizen with quick eyes and a toucan nose. The interpreter spoke accented, totally ungrammatical English and smiled brilliantly and silently after each torrent of words by the Mad Mosquito.

"I remember you from airplanes," the little man began. "I tell you the great poem of my life but you say nothing, just nod like an idiot. I think you are drunk then."

"We're both of us sober now."

"You wished to see me about which?"

"About incidents . . ." Alec looked around. There seemed to be no strong-arm men nearby, thugs who might be in the vicinity to protect the Mosquito against journalists. "Incidents of violence that have occurred when you were around." Very swiftly Alec mentioned the explosion of the emir's car, the shooting at the WEB, the fire at Ellenbogen's place.

"These are coincidences. A man of the dusky persuasion, from Chad I believe, was unfortunate enough to connect me with a shooting. He was a liar."

"And where is the liar now?" Alec refused to be intimidated by this belligerent midget.

"It is of no concern. You are safe. Bad business to annihilate the press. Other journalists then close ranks and stir up the public. No, killing is wrong. Maiming, however . . . But why talk of such things?"

"Why not? I thought terrorists liked to talk about violence."

The Lilliputian waggled his brow, and the translator shrugged by way of amplification. "In the end we are all terrorists. The president of Algeria, Boumedienne, he was a terrorist. Menachem Begin was a terrorist. Eamon De Valera was a terrorist."

"Did you or did you not make attempts on the life of the emir, or on Ellenbogen? Off the record."

"My dear fellow. On the record: If I wanted the life of the emir I would have it. Not for nothing do they call me the Iguana That Shits Fire. When I shoot I do not miss my target. As for this Ellen person, I know nothing about her."

Alec tried a new tack. "Whoever the person is who fires at people *around* the emir, why do you think he does this?"

"Maybe you should ask the emir. Maybe whoever this person is, perhaps he does it as a warning. To remind that it is not only a shah who can topple. That the people must be given more."

Alec nodded; the Mosquito was not so mad after all. "Tell me," he said, "are you acquainted with Steelhead?"

"Professionally or socially?"

"Both."

"We have met occasionally, away from the forums. He is useful. But a confused soul, like all Americans."

The music grew cacophonous. Alec tried to put another question but he could not hear his own voice. The interpreter rose. He leaned over to Alec and shouted in his ear: "We are exhausted by these interrogations and beg to be excused. Good-bye."

"But," Alec began, "can we meet again? Can we—"

"In my country," the Mosquito informed him over the noise, "we have a saying: 'Since when does the guitar pick the tune?' " And, giving Alec their backs, both men became part of the pack of dancers.

"Wait!" Alec called.

"Thomas Jefferson was a terrorist," the Mosquito shouted. "Thomas Edison was a terrorist. Joe DiMaggio was a terrorist."

In the next few days Alec quietly tried to find connections between Steelhead and the bombers. The best evidence he could turn up were several references in the ambassadorial speeches, allusions to oppression by heads of states. Steelhead was particularly hard on democracies. Israel was taxed with land-grabbing, England with class war, Denmark with indifference. His own country, he admitted in a press conference, was the hog of the global farm, swilling down the world's oil, steel, and sunshine.

"Why doesn't he ever mention Russia or China?" Through his glass Alec stared at the red sun receding behind the factories.

"Be fair," said Hackett. "How could he? I mean, there's arms limitation talks with the USSR, China's just opening up. Any place where they're knocking down the press and grinding the faces of the poor, that's the place we're setting up shop. Can't very well blast *them* and then hope to sell them things."

Hackett had thrown out broad suggestions that Alec go home early, but it was soon evident that Alec had nothing else to do, and that he intended to stay. After some protestations, Hackett grumbled an invitation for the Thursday evening poker game. As the infusions of vodka began, he became warmer and more convivial. Soon the other players began to file into the press room. Alec had never seen any of them before. There was a large, cylindrical woman, Irene Kass, from a Viennese newspaper, who wore yards of paisley. "The Guggenheim Museum in love," Hackett muttered. Two dark men with quick black eyes and matted hair arrived. They wore uniforms with no markings and sat quietly and impassively waiting for the game to begin. A huge Portuguese, almost seven feet tall, loomed in the doorway, went to a wooden chair, sat in it, broke it, and changed to another without saying a word. A British colonel with a face straight off a Toby jug came in, belching. A humorless old German couple asked if their house guest could come in, then brought on a tiny black man in a dashiki who spoke pidgin English and cracked Indian nuts with filed teeth. Alec found him oddly familiar;

he thought perhaps they had met years ago, in London.

The game began immediately. The kings and queens felt foreign in Alec's hand, part of the old revulsion. He recalled now how much he hated card games. But he stayed, sipping quietly at his drink, playing conservatively, losing small amounts. Only the Portuguese kept winning, piling up his chips in silence.

As the air grew staler and the hour later, the African guest grew more agitated.

"Dam card," he said. "Big fella belong queen come along too slow." He thrust his foot up. It met the table in the center and cards, chips, and money filled the air.

Without embarrassment, the German couple gathered up the fallen articles and restored the table setting.

"He means he hasn't got enough kings," the man said.

No one replied. Betting resumed.

"Na fine hand now." The African grinned wickedly. "Bad juju gone. Make plenty metal now."

"Quite," said the colonel. He reddened perceptibly, and whispered to Alec, "Ruddy cannibal probably shrinks heads back home. Look at him; delegate, he is. Voted for universal women's rights yesterday. Except for those three nurses last year. His tribe et them."

Alec dropped out of the pot and the others followed— all except the Portuguese. The ante was raised to ten thousand dollars. The large man raised it two thousand more. The African frowned at the chips.

"No good," he said. "Bimeby mebbe better. Ghosts no lemme get first letters."

"Aces," Hackett elucidated.

"No letters, no win." The African turned his cards face down and emptied his shirt pocket. Ten thousand-dollar bills fluttered to the table. Everyone flinched, waiting for another tantrum. But the little man only rose and threw his hat to the ground. He jumped up and down on it, muttering some inaudible imprecations. "Good night!" he said pleasantly, and walked out of the room.

"Wait! A word," Hackett shouted and ran after him.

The colonel, manifestly relieved, dealt merrily. Alec's hand was so unpromising that he dropped out and went to get a drink. He heard a strange voice in the hall. "I first saw someone do that in a Chaplin film," it said in flat London English. "Max Swain I think it was. Brilliant piece of business."

Even without an affirming glance, Alec knew; it was the African speaking. He remembered now where he had seen him: rehearsing a BBC production of *Purlie Victorious.* He was an impressionist; he used to do imitations of Sinatra and Louis Armstrong to amuse the others offscreen. The entire scene with the kicked-over table and the Swahili accent had been staged. For whose benefit Alec had no idea.

He stood hovering at the doorway, straining to hear, watching the two figures until they vanished.

"In for this, Lessing?" the colonel inquired.

"Me? Yes."

Alec rejoined the group. Hackett soon returned, wheezing. Fortunes began to shift. Now it was Irene Kass who won consistently. The others grumbled but stayed. This time Alec closely watched one of the military figures as he dealt hands with a negligent air. And this time, Alec caught the gesture. Magicians called it the Up-from-Under. His father used to practice it before a bedroom mirror for hours, watching his fingering like a concert pianist. It was a method of making the bottom card move to the top and then out into an opponent's hand. But it had always been used to favor the dealer. Now it was being employed to favor the player.

Alec was satisfied. In Stolichnya, Hackett had told the truth. This was the way Ellenbogen had become wealthy. And not only Ellenbogen. Who knew how many others here were on the take? What was the military man giving out the money for? Publicity, in Hackett's case, favorable stories, or the cosmetizing of some coup. The other journalists were probably part of the payoff. But not all the other players were from the press. The African had paid money to the Portuguese, for example. What goods or services had he supplied? And to what country? Grambling was dead wrong. The WEB was not Siberia. A journalist could not only gather a fortune here, he could make an international reputation, Alec decided as the last of his chips disappeared into eager hands.

4

"Transblende," Ambassador Steelhead was saying. "Transblende and gauge each probonate with brassieres."

"I *think* it's brassieres," Gross reported. "It may be Brazil's." He squinted through the telescope again. "You're sure he's not speaking in code?"

Alec adjusted his binoculars and looked out the windows of the Commodore Bland Hotel to the World Body, two blocks away. It had taken him a week to reserve precisely the right room, level with the ambassador's office, and another day to rent a Japanese telescope and hire a professional lipreader. But Gross was unequal to his task.

The ratty young man looked up, bit his left fist with long teeth, and complained, "He's looking away. I can't read him sideways. There's a course in profiles, but I didn't take it yet."

"You *did* take the course in regular lipreading. I mean, you had the biggest ad in *Commentary*."

"My mother bought it. I told her I should finish school first. But you know mothers."

"Yes, I know mothers." Alec kept peering at Steelhead, but the ambassador gave him his back. "Where do you go to study this sort of thing, Mr. Gross?"

"The Great Counterespionage Agents School. You get a diploma and a badge in ten weeks."

Alec guessed: "And this is your tenth week?"

"Eighth." Gross brightened. "Steelhead's facing the window! Ah! I can see him perfectly!"

"What's he saying?"

"That's what he's saying: 'Ah! I can see him perfectly!' He's looking right at me."

Maybe you should ask the emir, the Mad Mosquito had said. Maybe I should, Alec concluded. After lengthy telephone negotiations an appointment was reluctantly agreed to, but for an hour Alec sat in the emir's sterile waiting room, turning pages of *Petroleum Week*, the only reading matter on the otherwise bare magazine rack.

Voices sounded on the other side of the wall, but they were indistinct. Alec pressed his ear against the door. He recognized the voice of Hamid Daladan speaking French to an associate.

"His Majesty is cranky," one voice croaked.

"He has had an argument with his wives. This always happens in New York. Disturbing Western ideas enter their heads."

"Yes. I heard this morning mention of lipstick and voting."

The voices hushed as a third party entered. The floor audibly creaked under his weight.

"You have accomplished nothing." It was the cranky, unmistakable piping of the emir.

"Majesty, what has been neglected?"

"The women's wardrobes: were they delivered from Bloomingdale's, Bendel's, and Neiman Marcus?"

"They arrived moments ago, Majesty."

"Altered to my specifications?"

"Even now a tailor is removing the labels. No one need

ever know that the garments were purchased at Zionist firms."

"And did you buy a newspaper?"

"Majesty, the *Times*, *Post*, and *News* are not for sale, although I offered oil leases. There is a New Jersey weekly available for half a million dollars, but it has a circulation of only twenty thousand."

"How, then, am I to persuade the United States? How can I convince them that our nation requires the Trident?"

"It will be difficult," Daladan conceded gingerly. "My latest poll indicates that Americans cannot comprehend why a desert country with no lakes and no seaport needs a nuclear submarine. They have no idea where we would launch it."

"That's because they cannot see my swimming pool. If we owned a paper we could show them, we could persuade, convince."

"Perhaps I might suggest," Daladan began tentatively, "Americans buy newspapers to keep from thinking. Of their marriages in the morning. Of their commute in the evening. Television, on the other hand, reaches their souls. If they have any."

"Then go out and purchase television."

"A set, Majesty?"

"A network."

"Alas, even to acquire a single station is impossible. There are unfortunately stupid laws."

"Then go out and buy me a television journalist."

"Majesty, this is not the Middle East. It is not even France."

"Yes. True." The emir's tone changed from acrimonious to regretful. "Yes. Yes. It is the trouble with losing touch with one's roots. I should have realized, Daladan. One cannot buy a journalist in America. Go out and rent me one."

"A news person awaits in the outer room even as we speak, Majesty."

"How long has he been kept waiting?"

"One hour, Majesty."

"Go out and tell him he may enter in two more hours. Then let him Zionist you down to one hour. You have to haggle with these natives."

"Yes, Majesty." Daladan advanced to the door. "Mr. Lessing? I have splendid news! I—Majesty, he seems to be gone."

Grambling looked up from his papers. "Be with you in a minute."

"I've been here forty minutes." Alec hesitated in the doorway.

"So? You'll wait forty-one minutes. The accountant doesn't like my expense account. "Go on, Matsuru."

Alec watched a small, scholarly Oriental advance crabwise toward Grambling, holding papers.

"Many questions." He shook his head. "On your December expense account you say dinner, Joseph Conrad. Joseph Conrad, he dead."

"Not *that* Joseph Conrad. The one in the Detroit bureau."

"He also dead."

"That's right. He was the coronary in the last fiscal quarter. Make it Henry James. The anchorman in Houston."

"This item? Cheryl, Irvette, Shoshona. Nine hundred dollars."

"The Cincinnati Bimbos."

"Name of team again, please?"

"It's not a team, it's what they are. For the cameramen's party. Listen, Christmas only comes once a year."

Matsuru frowned. "And the Panamanian rioters? Also not a team?"

"No. The *Morning Paper* said there was a demonstration outside the embassy. We got there too late. So we staged our own. Looked terrific on the special."

"Four thousand dollars worth of terrific?"

"All the radicals got Equity minimum. Plus there was the scriptwriter."

"Scriptwriter." Matsuru made more notes.

"For the placards: 'No Nukes.' 'America the Great Satan.' 'Death to NATO.' 'Feed the Cities, Not the Pentagon.' You think they make up that stuff as they go along? *Some*body has to write it. We got a Latin American poet, Rodriguez Montefusco, champion of the downtrodden. Cost us a bundle."

"And this expense: Eleven thousand dollars for snow?"

Grambling handed the accountant a small envelope.

Matsuru lifted the flap to reveal several ounces of white powder.

"The rock groups won't even talk to you without coke," Grambling complained.

Snow, Matsuru wrote. He got to his feet and retreated, bowing. "Snow," he said, shaking his head metronomically. "Rioters." Alec shut the door gently behind him, but he could still hear "bimbos" repeatedly until the accountant was a long way off.

"New man." Grambling's voice was full of refusal. "Now. What do you want, and why do you want it?"

Alec told him all of what but only part of why.

"A *bug?*" Grambling inquired. "You want to put a listening device in someone's office? Have you no ethic? No code?" He pointed to a framed motto on the wall: *General Wolfe's Five Laws.* "A Broadcaster," it read, "is Incorruptible. A Broadcaster is Loyal. A Broadcaster Obeys the Law.

A Broadcaster Uses His Power for Enlightenment. A Broadcaster Does Not Eat Sugar."

Grambling's index finger waggled as he directed it from the Laws to his listener. "The General opposes Tomism of any kind, Uncle or Peeping. I'm personally appalled that you would even think of it." He consulted a heavily embossed sheet of paper. "The General has just learned of a key meeting of the Third World Association. You know who they are, don't you?"

"No."

"Neither do I. Neither does anybody. That's how insidious it is. But the General called in some chips, so you can investigate. Thursday afternoon. Here's the address. Not a word to the others, you got that? They may be your colleagues, but they're our enemies. I want an exclusive for a change."

Even for Grambling, Alec thought, the outrage was too operatic, complete with accusatory finger, smote forehead, and fist over the heart. And on his way out Alec's eye was caught by the everlasting vase of silk fronds and peacock feathers on Grambling's desk. Doreen dusted them every morning, but still they gave the office the ambience of Bloomingdale's window. Surely there was enough padding in the expense account for fresh flowers? And abruptly Alec understood. In the iridescent eye of one feather a tiny microphone, smaller than a jewel, lay implanted in a vinyl scarab. Doubtless it sent what was spoken to General Wolfe's corner suite. It was exactly the way the chief of the network would bug an office. He was a very literal-minded man.

Long walks were an old habit, gratified by the boulevards and squares of Europe, but hard to practice in New York. In the first block Alec caromed off an old virago in bombazine who whacked him with her rolled-up newspaper and proclaimed, "Only Moscowitz touches me there!" He quickened his step as she escalated her shouts. In the next block he had to walk out in the street to avoid a crowd circling a black ventriloquist. Seated on a metal bridge chair, the entertainer balanced a dark brown dummy on his knee. "Do you know where Central Park is?" the thing was saying. "You don't? Never mind, I'll mug you right here." Near the corner four street musicians argued about the interpretation of Pergolesi's Toccata and Fugue in D, until one was stabbed with a piccolo.

Alec gave up and returned to the building. He stopped by a bank of pay phones. It would help to talk to someone, anyone, about the World Body. But who would believe him? Besides, everyone in the other, the real, the reported world was at work. No wonder journalists were wastrels; hours of down time when the rest of humanity was occupied. Who could number the reporters drinking themselves into afternoon stupors waiting for the Press Conference, the Cease-Fire, the Annual Report? Who could count the press corps of any nation who suffered from dipsomania, 3:00 A.M. frenzies, neurasthenia, hebephrenia, kleptomania, paranoia, schizophrenia, catatonia, herpes? The Fear of Waiting began to assail him and he doubled back, entered the delegates' lounge, and approached the long mahogany bar. He was the sole customer.

"Gentleman?" the patient old bartender said.

Alec turned stoic. "Iced tea."

Disapproving, the man withdrew. He had scarcely returned with the glass when Alec heard a voice above him. "Ah. Lessing. Good job you're here. Lintheads upstairs looking for you."

"That Moroccan from the other day? The stand-up comedian? 'Good evening, ladies and germs'?"

"No, this is a couple of goons in burnooses. Very serious. I'll have the same thing, Franz."

"Yes, Mr. Hackett. Another iced tea."

"I say, is that iced tea? Same color as Scotch. Better make it Dewar's and a splash."

"The same size as this, Mr. Hackett?"

"Certainly not. Just a triple."

Hackett lit the stump of a cigar and leaned toward Alec, exhaling smoke. "You couldn't advance me a tenner, could you?"

"I saw you win big money the other day."

"Ah. Well. Yes. But. I'm still over my head. Alimony. Child support. Orthodonture. Wish the kids had teeth like mine. Out when I was thirty."

Alec sipped in silence. He gave Hackett his back and moodily examined his notebook. Hackett reached over to an adjoining stool where a copy of the *Afternoon Paper* lay abandoned. The headline was an amalgam of favorites: "Porno Star Gunned Down by Six-Year-Old Blonde Aunt."

Hackett read with the intensity of a scholar. The *Afternoon Paper* was the scrapbook he had always meant to keep.

"Lived in Calcutta." His voice grew moist with nostalgia. "Saw people maim themselves for a life of beggary. In Africa I once watched a man with 458 children dub himself emperor with a plastic crown from Lamston's. In Iran they whipped thieves in the marketplace—everything just as it was five centuries ago. Except they amplified the screams with a microphone. Saw a slave market in Djibouti. Concubines, eunuchs, the works. I contracted photographers in Hong Kong and syphilis in Khartoum. Those were the days when you could keep it." His eyes grew dreamy. "Covered nine wars and eleven assassinations. God! Kidnappings, kneecappings, hijackings. We had them all." He banged down his glass and wiped his lips. "Thought I'd have the devil's own time adjusting when they assigned me to New York. But not a day goes by without five or six atrocities." Hackett improved the flavor of his cheroot with another triple. He smiled warmly. "And they say this is a cold town."

Alec, raised on these streets, watched the bartender polish steins with a faded blue cloth and said nothing. The town belonged to others now; Hackett was the surefooted Sherpa, and Alec was the climber. He could not recognize the cast in those zoo stories offered by the *Afternoon Paper*: the packs of feral children; the undertow of racial fury and envy; the degradation of the old; the dilapidated institutions. He was assured by columnists and intellectuals that the sprayed whorls in the subway cars were expressionist cries of "I Am," but to him they were death threats written in the international language of Krylon. Life signs, he was told when he walked around the sidewalk hustlers and the bag ladies and the furtive gibbering derelicts of upper Broadway. But increasingly it seemed to him that in his absence a city had fallen. There were to be no more civilities, no tacit understanding among the millions of separate souls who clogged the sidewalks and the stores. The old chaos once had an odd humor to it, some tenuous connection to the streets of Europe at whose docks the same Atlantic lapped. Today there were different forces at work, called by all the villainous names of the past: barbarism, vandalism, savagery.

The body of the People are generally either so dead that they cannot move, or so mad that they cannot be reclaimed.

Nothing new; Halifax had felt it, three hundred years before. Little had really changed except the scenery.

"Refill?"

Alec nodded.

It was brought by a new, young bartender with a plastic pin labeling him as Mark. Franz was at the other end, serving the Rumanians. They were berating him for putting too little paprika in their Manhattans. Mark leaned his elbows on the bar and scratched the inch and a half of forehead abbreviated by red woolly curls.

"Either we get them or they get us," he announced.

"Who?"

"Who? Them." He turned his own *Afternoon Paper* around to give Alec a better look. The Greek Embassy in Madrid was occupied by Turks. In Dublin, a troop of radical Palestinians goose-stepped past the British legation. A Soviet militia threaded through the streets of what was once Armenia while children dropped rocks from the roofs. Bolivia announced plans to test a neutron bomb in the deserts of Honduras. South Africa had replaced a thousand diamond miners with four categories of cybernetic devices: symbiotic, analogue, colored, and black. The newest non-aligned nation of Chren, four hours old, demanded that the United States pay a hundred dollars to every Chrenedian man, woman, child, and bullock in order to redress the imbalance of centuries-old imperialism.

"I'm telling you," Mark said, but added nothing.

Alec shrugged and went back to his notebook. The bartender served a party of Sikhs and returned to Alec.

"I'm like Noah," he said. "I warn. People think they got better things to do. Meanwhile, the clouds line up. How long can they go with their atomic collectibles, these characters? Sooner or later, somebody's going to drop the big one."

Alec slid off the bar seat, too late. Mark reached down to a shelf for some pamphlets. "I'm only working here until the apocalypse," he explained. "Then I'm moving to Baja California."

Alec turned to Hackett. In what he hoped was a disinterested voice he asked, "Do you know anything about Steelhead's secretary? Dale Knowles?"

Hackett's face was hidden by the paper. "A little."

"Good-looking?"

Hackett remained buried in a story concerning cannibalism on Staten Island. He had to be asked twice. Then, as he examined a fly on the rim of his drink: "Not bad."

"Married?"

"No. Used to live with a ballplayer."

"Young?"

"Only the hair. Gray roots. Uses too much scent."

"Not your type."

"I don't dare philander. I always marry them, you see. I—"

But Alec had already departed. Hackett, hiding a vulpine smile, went back to his rapists and slashers.

As Alec approached the press room two cumbrous men in traditional attire approached him.

"Mr. Lessing?"

"Yes."

"We are from the emir. He sends his blessings."

"I send mine."

"He wishes to see you."

"And I him."

"Now."

"All right. Let me check with my office, and then—"

"The check will be unnecessary," said one.

"You will oblige us by riding in our taxicab," the other added.

"I'll get my own cab, thanks."

"Ours is nicer." The larger one ostentatiously reached

into his robe. Alec had not known that one could carry a rifle in such a garment.

"Yours is nicer," he agreed.

They might have walked faster. The car, a white hardtop driven by another large man in a burnoose, inched north between pedestrians, Con Edison repairmen, and construction sites. Fire engines shrieked and bellowed across town. At Fifty-seventh Street, picketers held up traffic while television cameras recorded their angry chants. At one corner, placards asked for donations to save the whales, but they were soon outshouted by women dressed as soldiers and men in organdy gowns. It was Transvestite Pride Day.

The emir's apartments took up the second through seventh floors of a dignified structure on Fifth Avenue.

A stern, turbaned official guided Alec up flights of stairs carpeted in a familiar pattern. In an old apartment, decades ago, the living-room rug had displayed the same sworls and shades of magenta, yellow, and ochre. He imagined in those days that the magenta was eternal fire, and that if he slipped from the safe grid of ochre he would be consumed. The old dread returned and Alec walked in the same juvenile pattern, one foot cautiously put before the other until he arrived at the top landing.

The emir gave a sharp command to the men. When they vanished into side rooms he switched to his own brand of English.

"Ah!" he said, extending a moist warm hand. "Welcome. What a great 'kick' to see you."

Alec looked past his host at the surroundings. He had expected a palatial layout; something on the order of Ellenbogen's interior but designed with more petrodollars and informed with the taste of a name decorator. Instead, he saw the plainest white ceilings and walls, no statuary, no paintings, bare polished floors, and a minimum of light fixtures. It resembled the spartan quarters of those leaders who denied themselves creature comforts until their people were adequately sheltered and nourished. Out of view, on the fifth through seventh floors, were the Empire and Biedermeier furnishings, the walls of Renoirs and Derains and Bonnards, the Aubusson carpets and T'ang vases. But, in fact, the emir had no love for those Western objects. His accountants and advisers had purchased them only for investment, acquired at auctions and at distress sales held in the Fifth Avenue apartments of widows who needed ready cash. The emir preferred this floor with its absence of array, far from the wives and Impressionists. It was here that he got his best fomenting done.

"Come," he said. "Sit down and 'let it all hang out.' "

Alec chose a hard maple chair. It scraped on the parquet when he sat down. The emir preferred a leather hassock. He regarded his guest.

"Americans," he said warmly. "So tall. So healthy. The result of 'three squares' a day." He pulled the hassock closer. Alec detected an aromatic blend of sandalwood and Right Guard.

"I love 'the States,' " the emir continued. "Of course, you have your portion of 'jive turkeys.' Who has not? But I am made comfortable here."

"Yet you have been attacked," Alec reminded him. "Shot at."

"It is unfortunate. Abuse cannot be spelled without U.S.A. But then, what nation is without faults? My own country, for example, has many flies."

As the emir burbled, Alec looked around. He searched the moldings, the light fixtures, and the furniture for obvious bugs. There were none. Still, there might be that ancient device, the human ear, leaning on the doors, or even the wall, against an inverted tumbler. That was probably the way they did it in the old country.

The emir had finished speaking about his nation's new air force, his heat-seeking anti-aircraft system, his crack troops. Now he was extolling the country's second biggest industry, after oil: sand. It was used for abrasives and glass, it could be sat on, it could fill bags in case of revolution, it could be placed in hourglasses to tell time. It could be used in cement, and at the beach.

The travelogue issued from a mouth shaped like a pitcher's, with a large, moist lower lip, and a small, efficient upper one. Alec watched it slow down; he now began to fidget. No real threat issued from this round, oleaginous figure, but people around the royal presence had a habit of getting shot at, or blown up.

"You will, of course, 'chow down' with me." The emir clapped his hands twice. The doors abruptly swung open and a servant appeared at Alec's back.

"Majesty?"

"What is your pleasure?" inquired the host. "We have all things."

Not quite, Alec thought. You don't have me. One lobe of his brain urged him toward the door, to get out before the next attempt at the emir's life. The other lobe wanted him to stay, to learn what an impoverished WEB correspondent could do for the man who had everyone.

"Just tea," he said.

"The same," instructed the emir. "And some of those 'dynamite' cakes from 'Bloomie's.'"

The refreshments were wheeled in by Hamid Daladan, dressed in a Western suit, smiling with great benignity. He listened, as deferential as a shadow. The emir dilated about sand, about highways, vertical takeoffs, and air-conditioning. Suddenly the speaker stopped himself, introduced his assistant to Alec, and said, "What kind of absolute monarch am I to go on and on about myself? What of you?"

"You didn't invite me here to ask about my biography," Alec responded. "You want something."

Silence. Very gradually the emir's stiff face allowed itself a grin, then wrinkled into merriment.

"Admirable," he laughed. Daladan echoed the regal mirth. "So direct. So honest. A 'built-in bullshit detector.' "

But Alec did not join in the merriment. That disturbed the host.

"You are displeased?" he concluded. "Is it the tea? Sometimes the A & P 'house brand' tends to be—"

"It's not your tea. It's your invitation."

"Pardon?"

"Next time you want somebody, don't send two gorillas. Just call him up and ask him nicely."

The potentate glared at his assistant.

"Ten million apologies," Daladan offered immediately. "It was only our anxiety to see you. An excess of zeal."

"Why me?"

"My dear fellow, why not you?" The emir moved still closer. "I am told you are the newest correspondent at the WEB. Still idealistic. Unspoiled. This is what I want. Someone to help write a brochure about my native land. To dispel the outrageous lies they tell about us."

"What lies are those, Your Majesty?" Alec got out his notebook. Daladan grew restive. "Please. Mr. Lessing. Notes are not necessary. This is strictly off the record."

Alec returned the notebook to his pocket, but he repeated the question.

"What lies?"

"To begin with," Daladan said, "prevarications about our foreign policy."

"Yes," said the emir. "We have no foreign policy. I would 'nuke' anyone who says we do."

"Majesty, perhaps it would be better if I answered the journalist's questions." Daladan turned to Alec. "And as for the problem of slavery, this is a vicious untruth."

"Yes," said the emir. "There are no more than nine thousand vicious untruths working in the emirate now, and they will be freed by the end of the century."

"Majesty, please. What the emir means—"

"What I mean is that I should like very much to 'put you on the payroll' as a consultant, Mr. Lessing. Help us explain our difficulties, our dreams, our ambitions."

"I've never been to your country."

"We will 'foot the bill' for a round trip."

"Thank you just the same."

"Very well, a trip is unnecessary. We will supply you with facts."

"No thank you."

"We would be willing to pay fifty thousand 'simoleons' for your editorial assistance."

A little shiver passed through Alec as he thought about Azie and the price of child support, about rent, about manifold varieties of slavery, physical, emotional, and economic. Another shiver occurred when he refused. It was followed by a feeling of resentment against the tempters. But he sat, listening. Mischief was already lighting the corners of his eyes.

"Alas," the emir shook his head tragically, "we must look elsewhere. A pity. We need aid. We want so much to tell our story to your people."

"You don't want a journalist," Alec advised him.

"No?"

"The best you can get from the news is two minutes. If they do a segment on the Middle East. What you want is a sitcom."

"A which, Mr. Lessing?"

"A situation comedy. On prime time. Once a week for half an hour you could be telling your story to millions."

"Why did you not think of this, Daladan? Brilliant!"

"I even know a stand-up comedian." Alec warmed to his subject. "A very funny gentleman. I have his card somewhere." He produced it for his listeners.

"Magnificent!" Once again the emir offered a consultancy, a reward, a free trip. Alec politely refused. It was a pleasure to be of help, he said. When he rose the men did not detain him. The emir and Daladan accompanied him all the way to the front door and stood before it, in the open air.

"Good-bye," said Daladan, offering his hand. The emir warmly embraced Alec with both arms. "May I offer you a ride home? My new chauffeur—"

"I'll walk."

As Alec declined, he heard a mysterious and indefinable offstage crack, like the one in Act Two of *The Cherry Orchard*. There was a pause of about a second before an enormous cement gargoyle crashed down from the roof, narrowly missing the trio. Bits of stone lay scattered everywhere. Powder rose in the evening air.

" 'Holy cow!' That was meant for us!" The emir was shaken.

"An accident, Majesty." Daladan took his leader away.

A warning, Alec decided, looking upward. Although for whom he could not decide.

5

The first message was from the Third World News Service. It offered Alec an exclusive: he would be the only Western journalist to be admitted to a closed-door session at their offices at Mitchell Place. The second message seemed misdirected. Typed on a yellow interoffice slip was the unfamiliar legend *Call your wife.* Alec had gone wifeless for a long time. Laura must still think of herself that way, he guessed. Or perhaps she thought "please call Laura" would confuse her with other Lauras. She assumes I have a harem like the emirs. She always did.

He dialed her number. The animal answered and turned the phone over to Laura.

"Thank you for calling back." Her voice conveyed the relentless cheer of a catfood commercial. "We wanted to invite you to dinner Saturday."

"We?"

"Reed and me? It's going to be just us and maybe the Strykers? They're survivalists?"

"Is this your new voice?"

"What new voice?"

"Ending everything with a question."

"I just wanted to find out if you're interested?"

Alec tried to remember what survivalists were.

"*You* know?" Laura said. "People who believe World War III could happen any minute?"

"If it happens before Saturday night is dinner still on?"

"Same old Alec."

"Brand-new Laura."

"Bring a friend?"

He mumbled an acceptance and hung up, numb. Bring a friend. Meaning a date. Laura's way of defining maturity. You invited your ex-husband and his friend to dine with you and *your* friend. The past tense of emotion: Now we feel, yesterday we felt, we are feeling, we have split.

Briefly, he considered borrowing Titania from his father: "Pop, can I have the keys to the concubine?" But Laura would see through the masque. It would have to be someone significant; if possible, a bimbo. He thought of Steelhead's secretary again, Dale Knowles. It was short notice; still, the hours at the WEB were bizarre. She might be there. He took the elevator to Steelhead's floor and walked down the long blue-carpeted corridor, approaching the desk warily. He came within ten feet. She was still on duty. Dale looked fashionably haggard, in a tailored heather suit too conservative for her false eyelashes. She appeared prim but not cold, and when Alec asked for an appointment to see Steelhead she smiled with what he perceived as more than office *politesse*.

"Unfortunately, the ambassador can't make any appointment for two weeks."

Alec affected despair. He admired the pink-veined daisies on her desk. Was it her birthday?

"No," replied the husky voice. She had picked them herself from her windowbox and then put them in red ink.

"Inventive," Alec said. No reply. A book lay open on the corner of her desk. He read the print upside down: *Within a Budding Grove.*

"I met the niece of Proust's housekeeper when I was stationed in Paris."

Clamorous silence. Alec searched the desk for other methods of entry.

He could hear the hushed clack of a distant secretary working at her IBM Selectric. There were no other sounds.

"I . . . wonder if you could . . . Saturday night . . ." Alec began. He was interrupted by a buzzer. The ambassador was summoning his secretary. The sun was a sullen red: it might be nightfall before she returned. Dale might even exit with Steelhead. Hopelessly, Alec turned away when Dale rose from her chair, gathered her steno book to her small sharp bosom, and smiled.

"OK." Her voice was terse and decisive. "But no S and M, no leather, and you can't stay over."

The bus sighed and halted.

Hope is generally a wrong guide, though it is very good company by the way.

Alec put Halifax away and dismounted. He consulted his notebook again: Third World meeting, Mitchell Place, 3 P.M., Thurs. The address did not sound like something in Manhattan. But neither did Duke Ellington Boulevard, Dag Hammarskjöld Plaza, Jazz Street, or Fashion Place. But there they all were, scattered about the city, the nouns standing defiantly against the numbered streets and days.

Mitchell Place turned out to be a little thoroughfare just off First Avenue, pleasantly lit and elegantly situated, not at all a street where unseasoned journalists would expect to find the Third World Association. The organization had offices furnished in high tech: track lighting, metal desks and chairs, chrome and white plastic ceilings, as if the members had elected to live in a parody of the most depraved and soulless Western taste.

A guard in a gray paramilitary uniform motioned Alec in. At the rear of the room a set of double doors were attended by two Orientals in loose-fitting white kimonos with large black belts. They were related in appearance but varied in detail, like the frog and fish footmen in *Alice in Wonderland.*

"Your name and affiliation?" inquired the frog.

Alec repeated his name, but thought better of mentioning the network. A Slavic gorgon approached him.

"Emma Gryzynyk, director." She too was wearing a white robe, but hers was tied with a brown belt. "The kimono is not compulsory. It depends on your attitude. Kalua here always wears saris. But her mind wears a black belt." A tremulous young woman with brilliant dilated eyes came by holding a tray of tiny meatballs.

"I hate untruth," she said pleasantly.

"Me too," Alec told her, wishing privately that he had not invited Dale to dinner. "If there's anything I hate it's untruth. What I like is truth. It's . . . I don't know, factual." He speared a meatball with a red plastic toothpick.

"Facts are everything," Kalua persisted.

"Exactly. The world is made of facts. The way matter is made of protons." Or was it neutrons? He tried to remember.

"Then why are you a television newsperson?"

"Well, that's the whole point. Facts are what newsmen, newspeople—"

"The American recites fiction and calls it truth."

"Well, I—"

"Selling detergents to people who do not need them, blue jeans to little children."

"No, those are the commercials. People like me tell what's happening."

"You tell what the detergents *want* you to tell."

Alec reversed course; he was glad now that he had

invited Dale. The speaker, as he looked at her closely, was not actually beautiful. In fact, there was such a thing as cheekbones that were too sculpted, eyes that were too large, a mouth—

"Blue jeans." The mouth pursued its quarry. "These are to show off little girls' buttocks. We have a nasty name for it in my nation. We call it journalism."

"I wouldn't pay much attention to that," A twinkling old party whispered through a snowy mustache and beard. Alec turned away from Kalua, who continued to address the air on the subjects of soap and buttocks.

Alec introduced himself. The man said, with an accented tone, "They call me Old Man Winter." Conspiratorially he gripped Alec's arm. "It's not my real name."

"No, I didn't think so."

"They say you're a reporter. I, too."

A gong rang. The two men were hustled down a carpeted ramp along with the other arrivals, like oranges in a chute.

They came to an auditorium. As two more guards frisked them for weapons Alec inquired for what paper Old Man Winter worked.

"Not a paper exactly."

"TV? Radio?"

"Neither. You see, Mr. . . . ?"

"Lessing."

"Just so. In my capital we have a vast and complex system of buses and trains, you understand?"

Alec gave an uncomprehending nod.

"At each stop, in each car, there are posters advertising liquor, cigarettes, clothing. The people write upon these posters: filthy sayings, political slogans, names. I go around with this."

He held aloft an immense Artgum eraser.

"I expunge graffiti. Not all—only some. What will go?

What will remain? Whose name will endure? Whose will go into the Hefty trash bag of history? What political slander will hold? What will slip away with the force of my fingers? You see it requires the utmost delicacy of judgment, editorial as well as janitorial."

"Yes, I can see that," Alec was able to say just before Emma Gryzynyk appeared on the rostrum.

The small crowd stopped moving about and took their seats. Alec made sure he was in one of the last rows, near the exit.

Trenchantly, Emma opened the meeting: Hundreds of religious and political beliefs were represented here, she reminded the audience. Falangists, Marxists, Hindus, Charismatic Christians, Sufis, Shiites; followers of Bahai and the Perfect Master, Bao Dai, and L. Ron Hubbard. All desires must be attended; no faith, secular or theological, would be slighted. But, she added, it was impossible to give an ecumenical invocation. Vegetarians objected to the slaughter of a black goat; communists protested the presence of religious rituals; and the landlord would not allow singing. Accordingly, there would be a minute of silence during which each member would stand or sit to worship or deny the existence of the gods of his or her choice. Knees cracked in small detonations as members of the audience shuffled to their feet.

Emma broke the long silence by angrily reciting the minutes of the last meeting. A voice behind Alec hissed, "You getting all this?"

"Hackett! I thought this was an exclusive."

"Secrecy's the only way they can get anybody to come. Except me. I'm here for the Third World hors d'oeuvres." He cupped his hand behind his ear. "What's the old dyke saying?"

Alec strained to listen. "She got a ticket for double parking."

"Yes, that was last month's yoke-of-the-oppressors speech." Hackett produced a pewter flask from his jacket and took a swig. "Gin?" he offered. Alec refused, but a dark, angry-looking fat woman to the right of Hackett said "Thank you" and put the container to her lips. "You don't mind," she said. It was not a question.

"Not at all. Finish it. I'm not thirsty." Hackett listened miserably as the gurgles indicated the passage of his evening beverage.

"The Third World thirsts for its share of global resources," Hackett wrote in his notebook. "What is not granted them by treaty they say will be taken by intimidation. And who can blame them?"

"Any new business?" Emma inquired. "Very well, then, Topic A: Censorship."

Eyes brooded, voices rose with hostility. The word was repeated in a variety of tongues.

" 'Cen-sor *n.* (L., fr. *censere*),' " Emma Gryzynyk read from her dictionary: " 'An official who reads communications and deletes forbidden material.' "

Mumbles of comprehension.

"But who needs Webster's to tell us about censorship? Who among us has not experienced the government's heavy paw upon the manuscript, the newspaper editorial, the evening broadcast? Who has not, sitting down to the typewriter, felt the most powerful restraint of all: self-censorship as she begins her work?"

Grunts and nods.

"Lately, in many of our countries, there has been a relaxation of limits. Few subjects are now forbidden to writers, thinkers can express themselves with greater freedom. The censors are growing old, bitter, and useless. We have reached a turning point."

Applause.

"How can we of the Third World hope to manage the

news when intellectuals and cosmopolites can think as they please?"

Swelling rumbles.

"Where are the new censors going to come from? In the old days, they could break in on small newspapers, university publications, small radio stations. Then they could work their way up to the big dailies, the key TV stations. But today there is little chance to develop skills, to root out and expunge the subtle phrase, the pro-Western argument."

The fat woman belched approval and handed Hackett his empty flask.

"So I move," concluded Emma Gryzynyk, "that we found the Great Censors School."

The idea hung in the air like the last bars of a concerto. A pause was followed by an ovation. Whistles, stamping, deafening cheers. Lobbying began for positions on the faculty. Over the cacophony Old Man Winter could be heard nominating himself for chairperson.

"You name it, I've expunged it," he was boasting as Alec attempted to rise. One of the delegates, mistaking him for a member, attempted to buy his vote by offering a pint of rum. Alec refused and pushed his way toward a pay telephone at the back wall.

As he pushed the network's number, he watched Hackett intercepting the offer, putting the bottle to his lips, and pulling at it until the delegate whisked it away, raining drops of brown liquor.

"A free and mutual exchange of resources," Hackett mumbled as he wrote, "will right the imbalances of the past." He licked up the drops that stained his page.

Everyone was pleased by Alec's in-depth 90-second report. Here at last was something even Grambling could appreciate: the threat to his own job. Censorship, as he knew from his overseas tours, led to uniformity of opinion, centralized sources of information, and, worst of all, the elimination of middle management. There were other menaces—though none quite as dire—and Grambling kept a file on all of them: creationists protesting the picture of a fossil on the science report, politicians demanding equal time, ethnic lobbyists charging defamation. These were all filed in the PIRK drawer.

PIRK: The Public's Inalienable Right to Know covered a vast arena: what the victims of a small-plane crash looked like when scattered over a quarter-mile of runway; the identity of rock stars' illegitimate children; the name of the president's chiropodist; the location of Chad; the White House budget for silverware; the troop strength of Chad; the number of pollutants in $C^{12}H^{22}O^{11}$, known more generally as sugar; the chances of being mugged in a city of over 100,000 inhabitants; the chances of being mugged in a city under 100,000; the chances of being mugged in Chad; and now, the dangers of censorship.

In a rare public address, General Wolfe told the camera that although censorship was infrequent in the United States, he was a strong believer in a distant early-warning system, a sort of moral radar. He was particularly pleased with the moral radar; he had thought it up himself. At the close he said, "I want particularly to thank our World Body correspondent Alwyn Lessing for his excellent report." A thirty-second clip followed of Alec interviewing delegates as they exited from the Mitchell Place meeting.

"Under your plans," Alec held the microphone out to a delegate, "there would be only one newspaper."

"If that."

"And television, radio—"

"Controlled by the state for the state. Here it is just the reverse."

"And if a citizen dissented?"

"It would be like having an argument with your own tongue."

The frame froze on Old Man Winter. Alec looked closely at the picture as it faded out. The faces in the background were blurred; it was difficult to identify anyone. But there was Hackett: the blossoming nose gave him away. And off to the side . . . was it? Yes, the little figure of the Mad Mosquito. Odd. Alec had not seen him at the meeting. . . .

"Don't interrupt him," Grambling had warned his two correspondents. But when General Wolfe said, "A first-class job, Alva," Alex reflexively pronounced his own name correctly. Crow braced himself, but nothing happened. The General heard only his own voice. "Was it a tough assignment? I knew it would be."

"More strange than difficult, General," Grambling assured his chief.

"One man can make the difference out in the field. One operator of moral radar is worth how many anchormen? A dozen?"

"Twelve, General." Crow put in.

The chief executive went on speaking to the three newsmen and once again Alec experienced symptoms of an old European disease. For the last two years he had begun to look upon the great and the near great as monumental and failing television sets. As he watched they would gesture but no sound came forth. It was as if a title appeared underneath them: "We have temporarily lost the audio portion of our program but will continue with the picture. Please stand by." Or, "This is only a test." Eventually a voice would be made out over the ennui. "Has the letters department showed you the mail?" the General demanded. "I thought not."

"No."

General Wolfe displayed a large manila envelope.

"Do you know what program gets the most mail? The local news. And you know why? I thought not."

"No."

"Because it gets women where it counts. Around dinner time. When all the juices are flowing. The air smells of food. The environment is warm, pleasant, full of children's voices. Then we come in with fires, wars, robberies. Tends to make an impression. And when we do a piece that uses our moral radar, well, you can imagine the impact. Listen to this." The General shook out several pieces of Xeroxed paper.

"Alec Lessing has the nicest chin in New York. Mrs. R. S., Maspeth. Alec Lessing is too tall for the WEB and too small for basketball, but he's just right for me. Mrs. H. G., Hyde Park." More papers were consulted: "Charming." "Outstanding." And the General's favorite: "Cleft."

The sound dimmed again. Alec was vaguely aware of some more letters, a smile, of being called Alben twice, a promise of more air time for moral radar. A secretary came in with memos. Through the opened door Alec caught a glimpse of five meek, worried men with colds who kept blowing their noses. The secretary left. The General turned his attention to Crow.

Sometimes Wolfe's bald head remarkably resembled a lightbulb, and at such times he seemed to shed light and warmth. It did so now as it moved about the room, humming tunelessly.

General Wolfe had no confidants; that was how he had risen. Nevertheless, he did have an adviser: Mrs. Wolfe. She was a large woman in her late fifties, seldom seen in public, and never without a cast-iron permanent and an expensive and monotonous off-white dress that made her resemble a federal post office. Like the General, she had come from humble origins. They had married young and he had changed. She had not. In many married couples this variance led to separation. With the Wolfes it was the secret of longevity and happiness. When she made a suggestion about a dramatic series (Couldn't the soldiers have a golden retriever instead of that dreadful bird?) it became a hit. When she felt that a situation comedy would attract more attention with the introduction of a black fireman and a switch to Thursday nights at nine, alterations were made and the program took root and ran for three years. It was she who gave the final approval of specials and anchormen. The General was merely a rubber stamp. She had a fault- less instinct based on the inability to adjust to New York, a mind that remained as shrewd, as impulsive, and as mini- mal as it had been forty years ago in Sioux Falls. It reflected the national psyche down to the final points of IQ and political preference, and it saved the network millions in polls and research. All the programmers had to do was run their shows before her and wait for the nod or shake of the dreaded, massive head. Behind her back, the General's staff referred to her as *La Vache Qui Rit;* even so, they held her in awe. They knew where the chief's ideas came from. They knew that when he spoke of the Average Man he was talking about the woman he loved.

It was she, he announced, who had thought of the new assignment for Crow. As Wolfe harrumphed on, Alec watched his friend's face fall. Gone would be the season tickets to hockey, basketball, baseball, football, and soccer, the carousing evenings with sportswriters and farm-boy athletes with too much money. Gone the air-travel card and the cheerleaders and the big games and the all-night poker sessions in the back of the plane.

"So you agree? Good."

"Yes, General," Crow said, just ahead of Grambling.

"We're going to call your segment "Good News." A kind of coffee break, if you will, from violence. A different kind of moral radar. Features about people who do good things: rescue a dog, return money they found in a cab, run little leagues for feebs, that sort of thing. Can't miss, can it? I knew you'd love it."

"No. Yes."

"On your way out ask the Joint Chiefs to come in, will you? They're the ones with the steel-rimmed glasses and the boxes of Kleenex."

Grambling returned to his office, smiling all the way. For the second time in a week the General had not chewed him out. Alec accompanied the morose Crow to his cubicle and helped him clean the files of any reference to sport. Out went the baseball calendar, the football register, the messages from fight managers, from first basemen denying involvement with Quaaludes, from lesbian tennis stars accusing linesmen of sexism. Crow wiped the glass top of his desk clean.

"*Good News,*" he moaned. "Where the hell do you look for good news in a town like this? Fifty years ago, maybe. But now . . ."

"Pretend it's fifty years ago," Alec encouraged him. "Ask yourself what the great journalists did. The pantheon figures: Grantland Rice, Damon Runyon, Walter Winchell."

Crow paused, holding his dustcloth in one hand and his chin in the other.

"You're right," he said, finally. "It may be a different time in New York, but it's not too late to follow the tracks of the masters. I'll do what they did." His voice brimmed with resolve. "I'll make it all up."

Dale Knowles was ready when Alec called. She was a bit aloof at first; the manner seemed to go with her foundation and blusher and her pearl-gray knitted suit, an outfit more appropriate to the office than to Saturday night. But in the cab on the way over she seemed to show evidence of the coquette. Alec edged closer to her and she did not move away. Still, he thought better of making heavy advances just before greeting Laura. There would be time later on for all that. He decided to appear dispassionate and ironic, with his detached and elegant date: something out of Noel Coward. Besides, her scent was unattractive. Strange how the same perfume would smell different on different women. On Rose it would be loamy, on Laura astringent. When he tried to explain tonight's peculiar cast to Dale she only shrugged and commented: ex-husbands, lovers, stepchildren—there were no rules any more, no moral parameters. She sounded for a moment like General Wolfe and she looked like . . . what? Alec could not say. Something eerily familiar, like an obscure actress from the Late Show. Impossible; he would have remembered the picture, if not the name. Besides, she was too young.

Laura made a point of greeting them warmly, making a great fuss over the gift bottle of Pinot Chardonnay, of kissing Alec on the cheek in aunt-like fashion and brightly parading him and his date before the animal and the other couple, Ken and Barbie Stryker.

The conversation went from red to amber to green.

"Basically, there are four models to choose from," Barbie said. She passed around an artist's rendering of various dwellings. Alec pretended to examine one, but he kept appraising Laura when she was off guard and everyone else was looking at the pictures.

He was distressed to see that she appeared happy. But every so often, when her face was turned away from the light, he thought there were signs around the mouth and eyes of disappointment or fatigue.

Stryker was a small young man, of great seriousness,

obviously used to addressing large groups. He was having trouble adjusting voice and approach to his five listeners.

"Can you all hear me in the back?" he asked. "Now we call these models our basic quartet. Of course you can mix and match depending on your income and life style. Now this"—he held up a blueprint of a square dwelling—"is the Pablo Picasso. Sleeps six. Holds enough of your basics, dried food, cans, bottled water, for three months. You'll note the photomural of San Francisco or the city of your choice. The bookshelves—"

"What's on them?" Alec leaned in for a closer look.

"Carefully selected volumes of your essential philosophers: Plato and Aristotle, Kant, Kahlil Gibran . . ."

He lectured away. Laura came over and poured more wine in Alec's glass. "Very attractive lady. Looks familiar."

Alec had a scenario prepared, but when Laura addressed him he told the truth. "Just someone I picked up in the office. I hardly know her."

"Not your type, I would have thought."

"Likewise." Alec looked at the animal.

"How old is she?"

"I don't know. About twenty-eight, I guess."

"Maybe it's like the ages of cats and dogs," Laura whispered. "You have to multiply it by something."

She moved to refresh the speaker's drink, a pink, ostentatious mixture of Perrier and bitters.

"Now this is the Walt Disney," Stryker explained. "A child-centered structure. Bunk beds, videotapes of *Pinocchio* and *Nature's Half-Acre,* all the essential nonsexist toys: Play-Doh, Lincoln Logs, bendable rubber grandparents available in white, black, Oriental or Hispanic."

"Why are the houses just one big room?"

Stryker turned to Alec. "It's the least expensive subterranean structure."

"You mean under the earth? Like a worm? Away from the sunshine?"

"Of course. You wouldn't want to be at ground zero on Doomsday."

Alec nodded mechanically and gulped his drink.

"The neutron bomb," Stryker said, "or the plain old hydro. Doesn't really matter."

"I guess not." Alec scratched his head. "Have you got anything in cement block? For the sportsman? You know, highlights of all the superbowls? Fifty years of the World Series on videotape? Something to do during the fallout."

Stryker proudly offered a new blueprint. "Matter of fact, we do have the Olympic II. It's got an indoor track: 416 laps equal one mile; plus films of the top milers, a mini pole vault, a mural of the Olym—" He was abruptly aware that Alec was glancing wickedly at Laura. "I don't know about you." He put the blueprint down. "But I don't think there's anything amusing about megadeaths."

"Well, it depends on your point of view," Alec informed him. "Below sea level I can see that it would get pretty stuffy. But up here, in the trees . . ."

Laura announced that dinner was ready. Her tone was grim. The subject was dramatically shifted to discussions of Dale's job. Dale spoke with a canny amalgam of respect and salinity. It may be, she admitted, that the ambassador was a bull who brought his own china shop with him, but he had several redeeming faults. The animal leaned across the table and out of the side of his bearded and mustachioed mouth confided to Alec, "Nice. I didn't think you went that way." He attacked his soup and rendered it senseless. Alec looked up, disturbed, and caught Dale speaking with animation, moving her spoon, the jaw catching the candlelight in a new way, again recalling someone or some place. She had been reminding him of an elusive, irretrievable incident all night. Now, as the Strykers laughed at a remark,

Alec suddenly saw her addressing a larger group somewhere in the city. Oh my God! He downed his wine in a
gulp and poured himself another glass and downed that.
No wonder Dale looked familiar. Oh God! he thought,
almost inhaling his next draught of Chablis, I wonder
if anyone besides the animal recognized her? But he knew
the answer: Everyone did. All the press corps, hence their
furtive, mocking smiles; Hackett knew and buried his
laughter in booze. Oh God, oh God! Ambassador Steelhead
knew; it was probably his idea to hire her: a new minority
to champion. The animal was now whispering to Laura,
noisily uncorking another bottle. Alec drank most of it before Dale finished speaking. Now he was absolutely certain
of where he had seen his date. He was in a taxi, it was
Transvestite Pride Day, and she was one of the principal
speakers.

"What is it in your memory?" Crow asked as the camera moved in for a two shot.

"It is forever etched," said the glowering adolescent.
Alec wanted to strangle him but the effort of rising to turn
off the set was too great. Clocks gonged in his stomach. The
blood drained out of his head and back to a less demanding
region near his liver.

"I will never forget the kindness of this man," the
insufferable youth went on. A fortyish minister turned his
glowing, sexless smile on the audience.

"Reverend Molument, how did you get Ernie to go
straight, to renounce his life of rape and mugging?"

"By introducing him to the one person who would
understand the depths of the criminal mind: a publisher.
Next spring, Ernie's memoirs . . ."

Alec recognized Reverend Molument immediately.
Crow was too shrewd to hire professional actors to appear

on his four-minute segment as victims and saints. For his first show he had gone to the Ab-Mal Pizzeria on Columbus Avenue to hire the co-owner, Harvey Abramowitz. The boy was his son, Morton. There were 950 stores in the immediate vicinity of Crow's apartment; it would be a long time before he ran out of good news.

"Now what?"

Alec reached out and made counter-clockwise motions with his right hand.

"You can't turn me off. I'm not a channel. I'm real life," the small voice instructed.

"Hello, Azie." He waved with his other hand and heard the rustle of paper pinned to his severely rumpled jacket. "Do Not Disturb Daddy," it said. "He is Sick."

Azie read the note. "Are you sick?" she inquired. "Or just hung? Why did you sleep over?"

"Why aren't you in school?"

"It's Sunday."

"Oh." He rolled over and looked at his watch. Noon. "Where's Mom?"

"Visiting Grandma."

"Why aren't you with her?"

"I'm supposed to be minding you. *Are* you sick? Are you just—"

Alec rose warily. "Did she tell you what happened last night?"

"She said you brought a man dressed like a woman."

"I . . . thought it was a costume party."

"Mom said." Azie now asked the question that had been tormenting her all morning. "What did you come dressed as?" The tone was bright with hope. "A rabbit?" They were still on rabbits in Calhoun.

"No, Azie." He could see the disappointment in her eyes. "I made my farewell appearance as a clown."

6

"Very dangerous." The old man pushed another log on the fire and the air-conditioner groaned.

"But vital," Alec insisted.

"Flagrant," maintained the Wizard.

"Granted," Crow conceded.

"Nefarious."

"I know."

The wood banged. Sparks shot against the fire screen.

"Also illegal."

"You'll do it, then?"

"Of course."

Alec and Crow had to interview almost forty performers before they found the one they wanted. Monroe Kleist was an afterthought of a man, an insubstantial figure with vague and furtive eyes.

"I bill myself as the World's Most Forgettable Person," he announced. "My mother don't remember me when I call home. They gave tests at Stanford Research Institute. Five minutes after I left the room I was described as six feet tall, five foot five, Haitian, Scotch-Irish, Korean. I walk out of here, tomorrow morning you won't recall what I look like."

He was correct. The next day all Alec could bring to mind was Kleist's porkpie hat and his red socks. Between, all was a blank, like Claude Rains in *The Invisible Man*. But right now, Alec had Monroe Kleist before him, and he issued marching orders: "Your name is Royal Jebbins. You're from Panama. Your story is you're an import-exporter and you have goods to sell. You're bringing me along as a client."

"What kind of goods I sell?"

"I don't know. Offer anything: drugs, girls, guns, whatever you want. Someone is buying something."

"Anybody else know about this?"

Alec shook his head. He had thought about sharing the information, but Grambling would give him a moral lecture worthy of Pecksniff—unless they spoke outside the office, beyond the reaches of General Wolfe's listening devices. Even then there might not be approval. Grambling tended to run scared unless the idea was his. The hell with Grambling. Let him yell afterwards, when the exposure was complete and the rewards were in. *Not since Edward R. Murrow . . . one lone man, armed only with the truth . . . international body restored to its original purpose of global peacemaker . . . WEBSCAM topples heads of state . . . these awards are not for me alone, but for the network I have the honor to represent, and for broadcast journalism itself. . . .*

"I hand it to you, Squire. A lot of men went that route. Dale's a familiar joke, kind of an initiation, if you understand my drift. An Afghani took her to three embassy parties. Fleischman would be dating her today if he hadn't talked her into going for a moonlight swim." Hackett was expansive. Alec, to show his good sportsmanship, treated him to an Upmann cigar. They were watching the blue smoke disperse as it rose toward the air-conditioning ducts of the delegates' lounge. Throughout the afternoon, journalists drifted by the table and traded winks, leers, and gibes. Alec was the soul of bonhomie, quick to take a joke, unwilling to hold a grudge. "Part of the game," he said, chuckling. And he waited agreeably for his companion to talk. As the clock edged past seven, Hackett did.

"Game tonight," he said. "Care to join us?"

"Who's us?"

"New crowd. Don't know a man jack of them. Heard about it at the gym."

"Sure. Where?"

Hackett wrote the address on a piece of the *Afternoon Paper*. The ink was furry and indistinct under the story of human sacrifice in Wilton, Connecticut.

A more manifest bunch of cutthroats would be hard to find in Macao, Alec concluded as he examined his cards. Except for the dozing Hackett, every soul looked as if he would slit your trachea for a Timex. Take Wong: the personification of Bret Harte's Heathen Chinee, long tensile fingers, with immense nails, playing energetic, quirky glissandos with the deck. To his left, Moshi Mweusi, an African of blue-black hue, aristocratic in bearing and capable of two expressions, contemptuous and disdainful. The MacKells were impassive Scots who yawned at their cards and bet a single chip at a time, never raised anyone, and dropped out with frequency, cursing their luck with pronounced burrs and saying "Ach, aye" if they were in for the next round. Across from them, a man of obscure origin, known only as Uhuru, who early in the evening claimed descendance from the God of Luck on both sides of his family, and then mimed with nods and shakes of the head for the rest of the evening.

Most of the participants had methods of bringing king and aces to the top, of concealing and burying whole hands.

There seemed to be no big winner, and after an hour the World's Most Forgettable Person attempted an opening. He spoke softly, out of the side of his indistinct mouth.

"Anybody here know how to move a thousand ouzos?"

The smoke lay undisturbed by the wind of response. He tried again.

"I got a thousand ouzos I got to get rid of cheap."

Alec vainly tried to signal the speaker.

Uhuru stirred. "I hate Greek wine," he said.

"Any reasonable price. Say three hundred dollars."

"At any price ouzo is too expensive." To underline his opinion, Uhuru shut his eyes and began breathing heavily.

"Why you want to sell ouzo?" Mweusi's frown creased his scalp.

"I thought you people were interested in Israeli submachine guns."

"Ouzi is submachine. Ouzo is Greek wine. Which you mean?"

Kleist was puzzled. "I don't know. Can I talk to Mr. Lessing here? Privately."

Alec studied the ceiling.

"Say," Mrs. MacKell said, dropping her accent, "aren't you what's-his-face?"

"That's right." Moshi Mweusi brightened. "I saw you in Savannah? Don't you remember? We were on the same bill: 'Mostly Music' at the Hilton? Corbett Monica was the comic."

Monroe scrutinized him. "Gooni-Goonie?" he offered.

"That's my name," Mweusi admitted. "Precognition is my game."

"Hell, don't you recognize me?" inquired Wong. "Worked the Spud and Push in Baltimore? Did the Canadian Buildup in Atlanta? We once worked the Staatendam. I was on B deck. Yo-Yo Chen, the Cantonese Con Man?

Two hours later and you wanted to be swindled again?"

"Of course!" Kleist sat back, happy. He knew the other couple now. "The Trent Sisters. Best counters in Vegas."

"Ah, well," said Millie Trent modestly, removing her mustache. "That was in the old days. They got guys nowadays with mini-computers in their jockstraps, right Mona?"

The sister discarded her burr. "Used to beat blackjack regular. No more. So we're back on the C, but only class stuff, no old ladies, no kids."

Monroe cased the room. "You mean we're *all* pros?"

The others looked around and nodded. "Except him," said Gooni-Goonie. He leaned over to poke Hackett.

"Let him sleep," Millie ordered. "We're working for a gentleman from the Wire Service. Who hired you?"

"Network," Monroe admitted, nodding generously to Alec.

"*Afternoon Paper,*" confessed Gooni-Goonie.

The Cantonese Con Man referred to his British Broadcasting contract.

Hackett snored on, ignorant, alcoholic, safe.

At the story conference, Alec tried to forget the World's Most Forgettable Person. He had not wanted to attend the meeting, but the emir insisted.

"This is my first 'story conference,'" the potentate reminded him. "I need counsel, advice, a few 'yes-men.'"

"I'm not very good at that, Your Majesty."

"You can at least listen."

"I can at most listen."

"Then I will settle for that."

So Alec attended. Watching the writers, he began to warm to his elaborate hoax.

The older, fatter writer, Huckabee, spoke first. "This

may be from the Seventh Astral Plane," he said.

"Go ahead," urged Trafe, his partner. "Recombine the DNA. Hit me with a new species."

"Well, what if we make the Moroccan stand-up comic here a visitor from the fifth century B.C.? He's been sealed up in a tomb and when they break it open to make way for an oil well, *voom!*"

"No mention of oil wells," Hamid Daladan warned him.

"All right then, a hospital or a whatzisface. A day care center." Huckabee spread his hands. "Out pops our friend the comedian. He was buried with a pharaoh. He was the court jester."

"Pharaohs had no such thing," said the emir.

"You know it and the pharaoh knew it." Huckabee began pacing. "That makes two of you. We're going for forty-five million people here. Now: Laughing Boy hits the ground running. Gags, japes, one-liners. Only they're five thousand years old."

"I like it," said Trafe. "It's got historical dimension."

"But I don't know any five-thousand-year-old boff-eaux," the Moroccan complained.

"Just apply the old switcheroo," Huckabee assured him. "You know, 'My pyramid was so small I had to go outside to change my mind.' . . . 'A hungry Mesopotamian stopped me on the sand. He said, "I haven't had a bite in weeks." So I bit him.' "

The emir leaned over and questioned Daladan in French: "Are you certain Huckabee and Trafe are not Zionists?"

"Absolutely," Daladan aid. "I checked their backgrounds myself. One of them contributed to "The Isle of Gilligan." The other wrote additional dialogue for Monday Night Football."

"Very well. But they sound like Zionists."

"Majesty, they may sound like Zionists. But they don't

write like Zionists." He raised his voice and addressed the comedy team. "This is unsatisfactory. What other ideas have you?"

Trafe scratched his cropped black hair. Then he brightened: "Well, there's Achmed Fixes the Plumbing, Achmed Finds Love, Achmed's Christmas Show."

"Achmed does not celebrate Christmas."

"OK, Achmed's Ramadan Show, Achmed's Vishnu Show, Achmed's Zoroaster Show, whatever."

"Mr. Huckabee?"

"He's Huckabee. I'm Trafe."

"Gentlemen. Our religious holidays are not meant for exploitation."

"OK, how about Achmed at the Singles Bar?" Trafe offered amiably. "Achmed and the Haunted Staircase? Achmed Goes Home, where he gets back in the pyramid and *voom!*"

The Royal Presence gave Alec a look of bottomless disappointment.

"Look, Your Majesty," Trafe said. He delivered a side of the mouth line to his partner: "I hate to call the sucker 'Your Majesty.' Makes me feel like I'm in the goddam Masterpiece Theatre." He pointed a finger at the emir. "Hey, Maj, what's your real name?"

The schoolyard tone left Daladan too shocked to intervene.

The emir gave his answer haughtily: "I am Ismail Nebuchadnezzar Abdul, Son of Abdul, Grandson of Mulmed, Descendant of the Planets and the Comets, Grand Vizier of Ancient and Hallowed Bakar, Overseer of the Holy Armies of Victorious Divinity, Ancient and Unchallenged Protector of the Shrines of Gamaze, Tiger at the Gates of Paradise, Leopard of Ushmir, Highest of the High, Mightiest Warrior, Slayer of Unbelievers, Circumciser of Traducers, Scourge of Treasoners, Benefactor of Nations, Sun to the Poor, Moon to the Crops, Water to the

Desert, and Serene Royal Highness to the Great Chain of Being."

"Oh. Well. Listen, Your Majesty, we can go either way with this thing. You want funny, we'll sweeten the laugh track. You want sad, we can put in violins."

The emir did not reply. He was engaged in thought. Beads of regal perspiration appeared on his upper lip and at his hairline. Daladan took a folding fan from inside his jacket and, opening it, tried to effect a breeze. The writers waited for the word. Distress appeared on their jackal faces. For the first time they realized that they might be ejected from the gravy train.

The emir gained control of himself. "Boys," he said finally, "I am not a writer. But I think you're approaching the camel from the wrong hump. The story is the star. We need someone we can care about, root for. We must then introduce a little jeopardy. Achmed doesn't meet a funny girl, he meets a girl funny, if you see what I mean. Then a ribbon ties it up at the end. The humor should flow out of the relationship. Think about this and return tomorrow."

The emir haughtily walked away with Daladan in tow. Alec accompanied the writers to the curb. He gave them the first taxi.

Huckabee turned to Trafe as the cab pulled up.

"You positive this guy's legit?"

"The William Morris Agency swears he could buy Connecticut tomorrow. They already cashed his check."

"OK then, but take away the sheet and the accent I could swear I was talking to Sol Berkowitz at Paramount."

"The people look like bugs," Azie was saying.

"Those are bugs. We haven't left the ground yet."

As Alec spoke, the monorail lurched and rose in a

gentle sway over the incongruous savannahs of the zoo. The trio looked down at greensward and outcroppings of igneous rock, bordered on all sides by faceless deteriorating buildings of the Bronx.

"I haven't been here since I was a kid." Shawna, Azie's senior by six weeks, refused to display any sense of wonder. Expressions of enthusiasm, except for the products of fashion, were forbidden by her dramatic coaches, her photographers, and her mother. Whether she and Azie giggled and whooped when they were alone, Alec had no way of knowing. All he saw was his daughter's best friend. Others saw a breathtaking ten-year-old with the starved cheekbones and the shaded, blasé eyes of a child model.

"I used to adore the chimps." Shawna pointed down to a nattering group of monkeys. "*So* much like my mother's husbands."

"Husbands?" Alec inquired. "How many does she have?"

"One at a time."

What I deserved, Alec reflected.

As they passed over the little pride of lions, Azie opened her mouth to say something, then shut it. Alec could see the delight drain from his daughter's face. "When is a miracle not a miracle?" he used to ask his classes. "When it is seen for the second time." The great seers, the true artists looked at objects and movements with the eyes of a child. But in this town at this time, children were encouraged to be amused by little, and surprised at nothing. They were not even supposed to be children. Commercials on the "Bugs Bunny Show" pushed flavored lipstick and washable blue eyeshadow to girls between the ages diapers and acne; Shawna Yates, a child without hips or breasts, was on screen every night breathing heavily into microphones, merchandising jeans and tank tops. Alec could see two old ladies in the rear of the car pointing to her and whispering. Shawna did not acknowledge them. She was accustomed to celebrity. At seven she had been the subject of a two-page spread in *Glamour*.

"Azie tells me you're at the WEB," she said to Alec. Her tone was that of a dowager making small talk with the doorman before the limousine came.

"I'm at the network. I cover the World Body. Maybe you've seen the 6:00 news."

"We're always doing retakes then." She looked down at the zebras.

Azie said, "They look like horses with pajamas."

Shawna turned back to Alec. "Azie has *such* a unique turn of mind, don't you think? She was the one who said when her leg's asleep it feels like ginger ale. *So* amusing."

"Mmm." Alec was noncommittal. Damned if he would be impressed with this prepubescent starlet. Probably controlled a conglomerate. There was a training perfume named for her.

"If you're with the network," Shawna asked, "maybe you know Delmore Witten? He's one of my mother's very good friends. I mean, *very.*"

"He's at the other network."

"Oh? How about Eleanor Marin? Joe Coyle?"

Alec shook his head. Full of unripe sophistication, flirtatious, Shawna lightly touched his arm, seeking a sign, an assurance that she had somehow bypassed the years of middle school to become, overnight, a miniature adult. He gave her nothing. She was his daughter's friend, a minor.

"Dore Persius?" she went on. "Frank Robie Williams? Leonard Hanes? Gregory Ellenbogen?" The car lurched downhill and the passengers reached out suddenly to steady themselves.

"Who did you say?"

"Leonard Hanes."

"After that."

"Greg Ellenbogen."

"You knew him?"

"My mother does. He took her to the ballet last night."

"Last night? But he's—" The car came to a stop and the trio filed out. Alec decided not to be led. There was no telling what this seductive child had in mind. She might have confused Ellenbogen with someone else. She might know somehow of his interest in the man who had preceded him, the man missing and presumed dead in a Canal Street fire. Or she might just be trying out some new allure beyond the perfume, the eye shadow, and the lipstick whose benefits she extolled. Maybe somebody told her to mention Ellenbogen.

Alec looked around. The new passengers were being loaded onto the tram, their voices as tumultuously varied as their summer clothes. Except for one or two gawkers, no one seemed interested in the tall man with the two girls. The tram doors closed and it began its journey back over the zoo. Azie waved up to the faces, rapidly receding, looking down. The sun hit the glass, obscuring the details of personality. But just before the tram vanished into a local jungle of oaks and plane trees, Alec saw the little grinning face of the Mad Mosquito, peering wickedly at him like Till Eulenspiegel after he has been hanged.

Alec stared after him, then shook the ice from his mind.

"Hungry, ladies?" he asked. They said they were. "Fine," he told them expansively. "We'll eat at the best Sabrett stand in town, and then we'll drop off Azie, and then you, Shawna. I'd kind of like to ask your mother a few questions."

But her mother was not home. Shawna busied herself with a mound of mail. "Jeans, yes, belts, yes, shoes, yes. Catfood, no. You ever do a catfood commercial?"

Alec had not.

"You open fifteen cans of Summer Chicken Medley before this eunuch comes over and licks your hand. It is to chuck upwards. You want something to drink? I'm sure they'll be in any minute."

"I'll make it."

"No, let me. Scotch all right?"

"Fine."

She vanished into the recesses of the place and returned five minutes later with a drink and a silver bowl of ice cubes. Shawna had changed from jeans and a blouse to a billowing diaphanous pink gown.

"You like it?" she inquired in a breathy voice.

"I've always liked Scotch."

"I meant the gown."

"I know what you meant."

"What are you so stuffy for? Dolores' father wasn't so uptight."

"I'm not Dolores' father."

"Too bad. He stayed over."

Alec had just decided that it would be better not to wait when he heard the locks turn. "We're home, honey," said a feminine voice, and Shawna's mother entered. Alec was expecting a larger version of the steamy child, but not this size. Mrs. Yates was an immense woman, a dreadnought displacing who knew how many gallons of water. Her legs, her arms, even her hair was fat. She had a small mouth, catastrophically enlarged with lipstick. Most of it disappeared when she kissed Shawna. Behind her was a small rat-faced man, smelling of tobacco. Shawna introduced them.

"I'm sorry," Alec stammered. "I—my daughter—I wanted to see Gregory Ellenbogen."

"I am Gregory Ellenbogen," the muskrat said.

"You couldn't be. I—"

"Ah." There was a broad, tolerant smile. "I see. I'm

Gregory P. Ellenbogen, the rather rodent-like Belgian emigré and film producer redolent of Camel filters. You want Gregory Z. Ellenbogen, the ambisexual and corrupt blackmailer and former correspondent. We often get each other's mail. I should say 'got.' He perished when the building in Soho went kaflooey. I thought you knew. It was on all the networks."

7

"You should have gone, Squire." Hackett examined the gold paper ring around his cigar.

"Who was there?"

"Nobody. That was the wonderful thing. Buckets of champagne, lovely cigars. And just me and Lopez, from the Buenos Aires syndicate. Trouble with you, Squire, you're too cynical. Lots of bimbos there too. But not for me, alas. I always marry them, you see. I ever tell you about—"

"Anything to eat?"

"Only their native food. Hearts of palm, I think. Or maybe wood shavings. Hard to tell. I only had three. Where is Junta Verde anyway?"

"I don't know. Africa, I think."

"No, they were all white."

"Central America? Middle East?"

"No. Very unpretentious headquarters. Ninety-fifth Street, East. Sixth-floor walkup.

"Walkup?"

"Well, it's an emerging nation. Principal export mung beans."

"Still, they have great hopes for tourism."

"Why yes." Hackett looked at his listener curiously.

"And they want you to write a brochure?"

"Amazing. You might have been a fly on the wall, Squire."

In the next few days Alec received two invitations to

receptions at the Junta Verde consulate; he threw them in the basket. So did everyone else, apparently. The events went unreported. Even Hackett stayed away from a third reception although the wire service ran a small story under his byline about the postage stamp-sized nation, favored by the Japanese Current, but only recently released from the yoke of colonialism. It did not give the location or tell the former owner of the yoke.

Alec was idly wondering about Junta Verde when he saw a small, vigorous man with a waxed mustache sitting in Hackett's office. The man nodded from time to time as he received instruction in WEB diplomacy. Alec leaned closer.

"Dunno what it's like in your locale," Hackett was saying between coughs. "But here sentiment is nothing; vocabulary is everything. You understand?"

"Onnerstand. Give me lesson. I pay good."

"Yes, yes, very fine. Now: What kind of breakdown is the military in Junta Verde?" Hackett opened his notebook and scribbled something in it.

"Please?"

"You know, color. What color is your army?"

"Olive drab, we wear."

"No, no, the soldiers."

"Ah! Privates black, lieutenants mulatto, generals white."

"Good. You'll get along here. When in doubt, vote with Brazil."

"Yes, Mr. Hackett. Very good. You instruct me now in . . ." He consulted a sheet of typed lined paper. "I cannot make out your handwritings."

"Vilification. Denunciation. Hardly any point in entering WEB without these." Hackett looked up, detected some motion outside, and ceremoniously closed the door. It was impossible for Alec to hear more. He returned to his desk and got out a small gazetteer. He could not find Junta

Verde. A larger map, he thought, and started on his way to the WEB library when the telephone rang. It was Rose.

"Alec, I have something that might interest you."

"You always did."

"Mel has a client, Mickey Moran. You know him?"

"Lots of Mickey Morans."

"This one owns a ball club."

"Oh, that Moran."

"That Moran got into some tax trouble this year and he just called in some debts. Guess who owes him?"

"Billy Martin?"

"Lance Steelhead."

Alec sat down.

"Are you there?" she asked.

"How much?"

"Steelhead is down for a hundred thousand."

"Crikey!"

"Exactly."

"Now do you wish you were back at Princeton?"

"Teaching?" he asked her. "When I can be a full-time blackmailer?"

"Alec, this is no time for ethics. This is the WEB we're talking about. Stay in touch, will you?"

"Can we stay in touch tonight?"

"No. Tomorrow after work we can stay in touch until about midnight. Mel started Tai Chi on Thursdays. Right after Group."

Dear Ambassador Steelhead:

It has come to my attention that a debt of some $100,000 is owed a Mr. Mickey Moran. I wonder whether we could discuss this at a convenient time?

Yours very truly,

Dear Mr. Lessing:

It is my practice to periodically grant interviews with members of the press. I see that your turn comes up next Tuesday at 3:00. Please be prompt. My schedule will allow seven minutes.

Very truly yours,

Billy's was chaotic; Alec could hardly hear himself talk.

"Crow, we have to talk."

"Talk excellent. Like meet fiancée Cindy Rice."

"How do you do, Cindy. Listen, Crow—"

"Cindy's on tomorrow night's show. Tell him what you're going to do."

"Talk celebrities," Cindy mumbled.

"Not just celebrities. Tell him what kind."

"Dead ones."

"Ter*rif*ic." Alec tried to intervene, but Cindy, having been put in the forward position, could not be stopped.

"Talk to Thomas Jefferson. And if there's enough time after the middle commercial . . . um . . . what's his face with the diaper?"

"Gandhi, dear," Crow reminded her.

"Listen, Crow—"

"I'll get another drink, Alec. Stay here with Cindy."

"No, I'll come to the bar with you." Alec and Crow pushed their way through the standees. Alec had to shout the business about Steelhead's debt into Crow's ear. His friend replied thickly, "Probably gambling."

"Why would a gambler owe money to an owner?"

"I don't know. Who cares?"

"Steelhead. He's giving me an audience in one hour. You know about sports. Tell me what to say. Should I accuse him of tampering? If I expose him will I lose a bigger story? Stop making faces. Listen to me, will you, Crow? This is big."

"All taken care of. Stop worrying."

"What's all taken care of?"

But Crow was no longer listening. Face down in the pretzel bowl, he slept. When he exhaled, little cube-shaped crystals of salt blew across the mahogany bar.

"How pleasant to see you again, Mr. Lessing."

"My sentiments exactly, Ambassador Steelhead."

An awkward silence. The violent city noise tried to enter the thermopane glass and expired weakly. Alec could hear his Accutron humming in G.

He pared his opening line to its essentials. "I came to ask you about the Moran debt."

"Ah."

The watch manically reminded him of deadlines.

The ambassador hesitated before inquiring, "Mr. Lessing, have you ever thought about working for the World Body?"

"No."

"Many opportunities exist for a clever man."

Those were the words of Ellenbogen, Alec remembered. "What would I do?" He leaned forward in a job applicant's attitude.

"Do? Obfuscation, circumlocution, denials, any number of things. We always need a good press secretary."

Alec's attention was diverted by a table leg.

The ambassador continued. "Embellishment, sham, equivocation—so many fields are opening up in the computer age."

"Thank you, no. Could we speak about the debt, Mr. Ambassador?"

"Mr. Lessing, I wonder if you celebrate Halloween?"
Alec was puzzled. "I used to."

"Perhaps as a child you went from door to door with
a little orange box, your face turned upward, begging
neighbors to give you pennies for WEBCO, the World
Body Council."

"Mr. Ambassador, I don't see—"

"Not only children give to this fund, which aids so
many needy people." At this Steelhead rose and addressed
some point in the middle distance. "Major businesses, cor-
porations, leading executives also contribute. But the con-
tribution that counts the most is yours." Now Alec recognized the tone; the ambassador used it every year on the
World Body telethon. "Won't you dig down now for that
extra dollar to feed the hungry, clothe the naked, shelter
the homeless. Our operators are standing by."

Steelhead's voice was so resonant and his manner so
entreating that Alec was afraid to break the telethonic
mood. He gathered his loose change and placed it in the
ambassador's open palm.

"Oh, wow, a dollar ninety-three, Mr. Lessing! No
heart too large, no hand too small." Steelhead took the
money and clasped his visitors' fingers. "The kids thank
you. The World Body thanks you. I thank you."

The ambassador's tri-weekly attendance at the gym
had maintained his varsity weight and vigor. Alec felt himself irresistibly propelled toward the door.

"Mr. Steelhead," he persisted, "you want to go public
with this thing?"

"Why not? I know it's only a dollar ninety-three, but
you needn't feel abashed. Every cent counts."

"I mean about your one hundred thousand dollar
debt."

"Oh, *that*. Moran overpaid is all. Ten percent of the

World Series went to the World Body. They sent us a check for two hundred thousand. Then they wanted half of it back. What else could we do?"

"The check was in your name."

"For tax purposes. What are you doing down there, Mr. Lessing?"

"Dropped my pen." Alec grunted and straightened up, elated. "Good-bye sir," he said suddenly. "Thank you for the explanation."

"Not at all," Steelhead returned generously. "We welcome press inquiries. Without a free press, what is the public? Savages."

"You called?" The Mad Mosquito and his interpreter stood in the doorway.

"Mr. Lessing, this is Mr. Escudero."

"We've met." Alec brushed by. He could only hear a short exchange as Steelhead's voice overrode the objections of the translator. "There's absolutely nothing I can do."

A torrent of objections reverberated in the background. The translator tersely threatened: "You must do something. The world stands at the rim of the volcano."

"The world always stands at the rim," Steelhead told him. "We will not negotiate with terrorists."

"Alas!" Voices chattered tragically, then brightened. "How about with nihilists?"

"No."

"Sociopaths? Maniacs? Fanatics? Mr. Ambassador, there is no pleasing you today." The door, protected by an air valve against tantrums, clicked shut discreetly.

"A transvestite and a teenybopper." Rose shook out her hair. "No wonder you're so violent."

"Too violent?" Alec asked.

"Not really. I just wondered what you were thinking

about when we were in there." She indicated the rumpled candy-striped percales.

Alec finished buttoning his shirt and tucked it in. He looked at his shoes and admitted, "I was thinking about last year's Super Bowl."

"Ah, *that* was why you kept telling me to punt."

"Rose. This time I know I'm onto something. I saw it under his desk."

"Saw what?"

"A bug. The kind the General uses in Grambling's flowers. Steelhead's is disguised as a ball-and-claw ornament on one of the legs of his desk. And I don't think he knows it's there."

"So? Who's on the other end?"

Alec rose and opened a beer bottle. He poured Rose's carefully, tilting the glass so that it would fill to the top. But he splashed his own until its head was larger than its body.

"Those microphones don't transmit very long distances."

"A home game?"

"I think so."

"Who does Steelhead report to?"

"The president, I guess."

"No, I mean at the WEB."

"He doesn't have a boss. Except—"

"The secretary-general."

Alec considered the possibility. "No," he said. "It couldn't be."

"Why not?"

"He's just a Scandinavian figurehead, a neutral. The *Afternoon Paper* calls him The Iceman."

"So?" Rose sat on her slender haunches, tilting her head upward to catch the remaining drops of beer. The posture elevated her breasts.

Alec came to her. "I'll look into it," he said, his fingers on her rib cage.

"All right, team," she advised him, "stay on the ground. Use your running game. Late in the fourth quarter you can throw the bomb."

Grambling was not in a conciliatory mood. "I don't give a crap what cockamamie scheme you hatched. I want coverage. We got three E.N.s this year and not one of them has been covered by you, I happen to know."

Alec had no idea what he was complaining about. "What's E.N.s?" he asked. All the words he could think of for the initials were obscene.

"Emerging goddam Nations is what. Jesus, you know enough not to speak plain English in here. You're in the communications business."

"You're talking about Isla Moise?"

"Which gave a reception and you weren't there. Also Chren. Also Junta Verde."

"I'll see them by this time tomorrow night."

"All three?"

"By five o'clock."

Grambling picked up the telephone and began a furious negotiation with the Writers Guild of America. "Go ahead and strike," he was saying as he waved Alec out of the room. "You could fit the whole 7:00 news on the front page of the *Morning Paper*. I don't need writers at all. I can do it with one guy who can make up fortune cookies."

The ambassador from Chren greeted Alec personally. He was a gracious, surprisingly tall man, Eurasian in bone structure and characteristics, educated at Cambridge.

"Welcome to a little piece of our little country." Alec was motioned to a couch. On the wall above it in four black Woolworth frames were portraits of the current President of Chren, its founder, Karl Marx, and Albert Speer. The ambassador anticipated Alec's interrogation: "You stare at the portrait on the right: Hitler's architect. A man before his time. A genius. He wished to construct an amphitheater: 'If people with different minds are all pressed together in such a place, they will be unified in one mind.' Beautiful, do you not think?"

"It all depends."

"On whose mind? The leader's, of course. In our case, Premier Duro. Even now, we are planning the stadium. It will house the entire population."

Alec opened his notebook.

"All three million." The ambassador warmed to his theme. "You have your Houston Astrodome. Your Seattle King Dome. But we will have our Chrenodome. Imagine: The first country entirely enclosed in a stadium."

"Mr. Ambassador—"

"I anticipate your thinking. We will require a loan from the World Bank. Yes. We know this. But imagine it: an air-conditioned nation. Who would want to leave?"

The video team, Pandora at the lights and camera, Boris running the audio equipment, moved through the room, their paraphernalia decorated with the customary *Save the Whales* and *I Brake for Lunch* signs, shooting reaction footage of Alec nodding vigorously as the ambassador spoke, and panning the walls and shelves for pictures and folk crafts: in this case two large steamer trunks, worshipped by the speaker's great-grandfather in the barely remembered days of cargo cults, and now supporting twin Betamaxes.

Alec offered the mandatory question: "What do you intend to do at the World Body?"

"We will not deviate from our avowed course: Greater recognition through the politics of embarrassment."

The ambassador smiled generously at the lens and the lights.

"Was it not Marx who said, 'Vilify, vilify, some of it will always stick'?"

"I don't think so." Alec dimly remembered another line of Marx's before the voice broke in again.

"Well, if he didn't he should have. As long as you're here, can I show you something in ivory, cinnabar, or jade? Makes a very nice gift for the missus. Very inexpensive."

The Isla Moisian embassy was another matter. It was situated in an elegant brownstone in the Thirties, the present of a high-minded donor. But inside, the radiators rattled and the paint cracked and blistered on the neglected walls. Here the portraits and photographs were of proud black men, whose fierce military expressions were given away by large sad eyes. The delegate, Ambassador Monon, was old, white-haired and somewhat palsied. The hands, with long expressive fingers and neatly-trimmed ridged nails, moved with his conversation, touching his dark-blue conservative tie, smoothing the collar of his starched broadcloth shirt. He shook his head. "Mr. Lessing"—he was the only delegate to remember Alec's name—"what I am here for is what everyone is here for: Truth. But I have no illusions."

Of all the delegates, Alec thought, this was the only one he had met who was not selling something: a service, an artifact, an idea.

"This is a dangerous place." He spread the large fingers across the green blotter on his desk. "You know the saying, 'The boys throw stones at the frogs in fun, but the frogs die in earnest.' "

Yes, Alec had heard it; he had taught it. The tenebrous bass voice continued: "We come here, a poor nation, re-

cently created of the blood of our people, sacrificed in the
wars of European ambition, and then, because of our own
fury and blindness, in civil war. We have energy but little
else. Only some minerals buried in the ground, along with
so many of our people: soldiers, brave men who knew that
they must die, but also women and babies." The eyes filled
and the ambassador turned away for a moment. Alec
looked down. The cameras gaped.

"What do you hope to accomplish, Mr. Monon?"

"Accomplish, Mr. Lessing? We do not accomplish. We
hope. We hope that somewhere, here in this angry city, the
cries for pity can still be heard. We want no hand extended
from guilt or from the expectation of moral recompense.
We cannot even afford that."

He began to rise, then saw the discomfort of the crew
who would have to scramble for new lightning. He eased
back in his noisy wooden chair.

"The Europeans came and made us their chattels. But
they taught us, too. We listened until we were powerful
and the Europeans uncertain and perhaps even remorseful.
We overthrew them and replaced them with our own
brutes, modeled after the Western caricature: strutting dic-
tatorial monsters, fat with influence, windy with talk of
Will and History. Glistening with power. Over whom?
Over our own poor hordes, driven from the farms to the
now barren cities. America promised us aid, Europe offered us advisers, the Soviet Union came with maps and
charts and methods to change our neighbors. We said yes
to all and meant not a word. Our leaders killed until they
were themselves overthrown. *C'est une vieille histoire.* Ther-
midor. It has all happened before. I am a remnant, Mr.
Lessing. I can remember so far back that the League of
Nations is not a fantasy. A time when one universal language would make war obsolete."

He fumbled through the pile of books on his desk for

proof: an Esperanto primer, still with its faded dust jacket, worth something now as an antique.

"Language, discipline, Bolshevism, the free market, the English-speaking peoples, the Caribbean Experiment, rifles, bombs, television, baby formulae, penicillin, rice, the return to ritual—they would all bring us peace. So we were told by one savant or another. But I, who have lived through it all, know better."

"Then why do you come here?"

"I am disappointed with the past, Mr. Lessing. I refuse to be disappointed with the future."

He was tired, he made a gesture of termination to the camera, but it kept whirring. Monon turned off his gooseneck lamp.

"Hey!" the camera operator yelled, outraged. Alec tried to restrain her. "Who the hell does he think he is?" Pandora's stage whisper echoed in the room and in the corridor as he hustled her outside, simultaneously thanking his host and wondering whether they would be on time for their next appointment at the Junta Verde embassy.

Boris struggled, puffing and clanking up the five flights of stairs on Ninety-fifth Street. Alec and Pandora waited for him. He cursed the stairs, the weight of his machines, the WEB, and the embassy.

"Gimme a war any time," he said when he reached the landing. "Ever hear of a battle where they had stairs? Say what you want about the Middle East. At least it's flat."

Alec knocked on the door. Only a small white paper, push-pinned under the peephole, identified the Junta Verdean legation. A cadaverous, mustachioed retainer, dressed in funereal black, admitted them. The place was outfitted with what seemed to be Salvation Army furniture. One armchair bore the toothmarks of babies and dogs. The lamps were of various sizes and wattages and overhead a naked light bulb swung on a frayed black cord.

An interior door opened. "Good afternoon." The speaker was a sleek, porcine man in a white linen suit. He fondled a white cat in the crook of his arm and stared at the visitors through round mirror-faced sunglasses. In another epoch, Alec thought, he could have played a middle-management villain.

"Please come in," he hissed, waving them through the door and into a large room. Here there were no furnishings at all, only six metal bridge chairs opened and arranged in a row. "You will forgive our sparseness. We have only recently come, and we are a poor country."

Alec introduced himself and his colleagues.

"Enchanted," said the fat man.

"And you are—?" Alec began.

"I? Yes. I am—" The speaker hesitated. "Excuse me." He opened the door to an adjoining room and disappeared, from which indistinct voices could be heard. In a moment he was back. "Call me W."

Alec wrote in his notebook. "And your title?"

"Title? Yes, title. I am—pardon."

Again he vanished and returned.

"I am assistant to the consul-general."

"Mr. W, can you tell me a little about your country?"

"There is very little to tell. We are underdeveloped, but of course we have hopes."

"I've been having trouble locating your country. Can you tell me exactly where it is?" Again W excused himself; again he returned.

"Make no mistake, Mr. Lessing. We are great admirers of the press. Not for us the censorship, the choking of free ideas. But we do not feel that we can confide state secrets to journalists at this point."

"But surely you can tell me where you live?"

"I'm afraid I can confide nothing more. Perhaps if you would come back in a month or so?"

"A month! But—"

"Good-day."

"Maybe if I could talk to your consul-general—"

"Alas, he is not here."

"Who's in the other room?"

"What other room?"

"That one."

"Oh. *That* other room. The cleaning lady."

Alec stood up and gave the others a signal. "Thank you," Mr. W," he said. "Perhaps in a month, then?"

"But—" Boris began.

"In a month," replied W. He pressed a buzzer and the walking corpse entered.

"See these people out."

Alec ostentatiously returned his notebook to a jacket pocket and quietly secreted his pen in a groove at the back of his chair seat.

They went to the door and stepped out. Alec turned craftily. "I forgot something."

W appeared at the entrance. "You forgot your pen," he said. The smile was tolerant; Americans, it said. Amateurs.

"Crow?"

"Alec?"

"Help?"

"Always."

"Embassy—"

"Which?"

"Junta—"

"Verde?"

"Yes."

"Mmm . . ."

"Plan?"

"Yes."

"What?"

"Secret."
"Legit?"
"No."
"Crow—"
"Bye."
"But—"
Click.

They gave Alec 125 seconds on the local news: three summary interviews and a comment the size of a cartoon caption. Monon was on the longest; the Isla Moisian was seen but not heard as the camera traversed the barren room and Alec's voice lamented the poverty of the new countries. Crow's segment followed a bank commercial and it was manifestly the showpiece of the night, the sort of segment that occasions thousands of calls and postcards and spins off into a show of its own. Cindy Rice of Lake Hopatcong, New Jersey, dressed in a discreet blue knit suit, sat on a tall stool, her long legs artfully crossed, her eyelids, enhanced with liner, closed as she communed with the beyond. She began as Thomas Jefferson, telling viewers that the Republic was "shaken, but not stirred." When Dean Steed, the anchorman, interrupted to ask, "What does the future hold, do you think, sir?" Cindy frowned and her eyelids fluttered. Clearly this question was not in Crow's game plan. After an uncomfortable pause she said, "Dynamite. America's future is very dynamitic."

Crow swiftly moved on to the architect of Indian self-determination.

"Mr. Gandhi?" Crow said.

"Call me Mahatma."

"Mahatma, in life you were known as a man of peace."

"That is correct."

"What do you think the chances of peace are in the world today?"

"Listen, everybody wants it, right? So it's just a question of getting together. I'd say the odds are, like, 80-20 for world peace."

Dean Steed broke in: "Mahatma, when you . . . passed on . . . your only possessions were a loincloth and a few personal items."

"Right."

"What do you think of Americans today, with our Cuisinarts and Betamaxes—when so much of the world has a per capita income of $500 a year?"

The tension on the set was palpable. Advertisers paled. But Cindy was prepared. She bowed her head and intoned: "Well, nobody really needs the Mona Lisa, right? I mean, art is a luxury too. Betamaxes don't cause poverty. Taxes do."

Alec thought he heard exhalations of relief but it might have been microphone trouble. The camera swung back to Steed and Alec turned the set off. He waited the requisite ten minutes until the show finished, then tried to reach Crow. But he was unavailable and he did not return any of Alec's calls that day or the next. At Crow's apartment the answering service asked the caller to leave a name and phone number after the beep, and the caller did, but still Crow failed to reply. No one at the office knew where he was. Out of town on assignment was all the information the news desk had.

Alec turned to other matters. He called Research and asked them for the current location of Bjørn Gruner, the secretary-general of the World Body. While he was waiting he called his daughter. Luck was with him; Laura was out and Azie answered.

"Want to go to the theater tonight?" he asked her.

"To see what?"

"I don't know." He ran his finger through the ABC's. Why do I sound like a courtier, he asked himself. I'm her father. "*Sam!* A musical of *Mr. Sammler's Planet.*"

Unresponsive breathing at the other end of the line.
"How about *Ape!* A musical of *The Origin of Species.*"
No answer.
"*Attila!* The Hun Musical; *O!* The Story of a French-
woman . . ."
They ended up at *Beowulf!*, the beast represented by
imaginative robotry. The tickets cost him $100 each.
Binoculars made the show considerably more entertaining
from the last row of the second balcony. At intermission
they came down the worn carpeted stairs into the lobby,
where Azie sipped overpriced lemonade.
"Wasn't that creature a hoot? Couldn't you just die?"
Alec recognized the voice, turned and saw Rose with
her husband. It was too late to look away.
"Hello!" he said, with bogus enthusiasm.
She introduced her husband, Mel. Alec revealed Azie,
obscured by two dowagers in unseasonable fox.
The men shook hands. Alec began to speak about the
performance as Rose, leaning down, inquired, "How do
you like those special effects, Azie?"
"A hoot!" Mimicry was one of her specialties.
A colleague caught Mel's attention and pulled him
briefly away.
"What a nice thing running into you and your date,"
Rose said.
"Likewise." Alec smiled as he always did when he saw
her unexpectedly, waiting for him at a corner in the old
days or jogging with the Pittsburgh Pirates baseball cap he
had given her worn backwards, catcher-style.
"Time for a drink after the show?" She touched his
arm. Azie saw the gesture. Alec saw that Azie saw. Rose
read his eyes. The combinations and permutations needed
a calculator, he reflected instantly. He had no idea what the
child would know or think or want from her father, but he
could guess that a rival to her mother was not high on her
list of needs.

"No," he said. "We're going to Rumpelmayer's for nine drillion calories and then home."

"See you later then?" Rose touched him again and went off to find her husband. The lights blinked, signaling curtain time.

"Yes," Alec said. "Later." But he wanted her now.

Azie led the way up the stairs. "How old is she?"

"Who?"

"The lady in the lobby."

"Rose? I don't know. My age."

"Three years older than Mom. And fatter."

"She's not fat."

"In some places she is. A lot fatter than Mom."

"Most people are fatter than Mom."

"Thin lasts. Look at Jane Fonda."

They found their seats. The lights dimmed. Alec tried to fix his attention on *Beowulf!*, on the set, on Jane Fonda, on anyone but Rose.

"How about those dwarves!" he asked as the spotlight illuminated the chorus line.

"Couldn't you just die?" returned Azie in deadly parody.

He could.

"Good evening. Dean Steed. Here now the news:

"Human rights were violated in every country in the world this weekend according to the World Body. . . ."

After the public service commercial for the laser show at the Hayden Planetarium and the thirty-second spot for a hemorrhoidal tissue-shrinker, Steed cued Alec. He spoke tersely about crucial events of the World Body. But it was all standard issue from the secretary-general and Alec knew it: a press release accompanied by footage of WEB officers clucking: ". . . as long as there are men in prisons it matters little which of us occupy the cells . . . Force is not a remedy . . . A decent provision for the poor is the true test of a civilization. . . ."

Even as he watched the news, Alec wondered once more how the WEB had managed to find violations in Junta Verde. How had they located the country? How had they been able to penetrate the ambassador's office? During the weather report he decided that he needed help now. Crow. But Crow was still out of town; Carolyn Brune was taking his place on the Good News portion, interviewing a mated pair of parrots on the formula for lasting relationships. Rose. She was good at dissembling, but she would be unavailable at the right time of day. If only Laura . . . A notion occurred to him. Very early the next morning he tracked Pandit to his new lair: a large space behind the word processor.

"Oh, my goodness!" Pandit tried to force his eyes open, but they kept closing. "Is it morning already? Where is the coffee lady?"

"It's five minutes to coffee lady," Alec explained. "I need a translator."

"I am not available. Oh no! It is against the rules."

"The network will pay."

"How much?"

"Double the usual."

"Ah, well, what are the rules after all? Merely man-made objects to be molded by common sense and opportunity!"

He extended a hand and Alec helped him out.

Presently the coffee lady came in and handed Pandit a fresh suit of clothes: an old arrangement. She served them both hot brown liquid that tasted of paper and acid, and baked goods with congealed margarine. Pandit went to his office, found a fresh shirt and underwear, and disappeared for fifteen minutes. He emerged clean and radiant, with the vestigial aroma of bagels clinging to his suit.

On the way to the Junta Verde embassy, Alec outlined his plan. It was punctuated by Oh, my goodnesses! from his listener, but there were no demurs. They climbed the stairs, Pandit shaking his head at every step. "This is very peculiar, this broken-down place," he observed. "No matter how poor the country, the embassy is usually rich." At the top landing he hammered at the door with a coin. Alec placed a package on the third stair.

A radio stopped. But no one came to the door.

"I know you are in there!" Pandit shouted. "I distinctly heard Johnny Cash."

Reluctant footsteps sounded within. Locks turned. The door opened enough for a narrow, suspicious face to appear. "We are closed," it said.

"Nonsense! Embassies and legations are never closed. I am from the World Body. Let me in!" Pandit repeated his message in seven languages. The onslaught impressed the man at the door. He allowed it to open. Alec followed Pandit in.

"We've met before," Alec reminded the Junta Verdean.

"Yes, the journalist. I remember." He turned away with theatrical disdain and addressed Pandit: "Alas, everyone is away."

"For how long?" Alec asked.

The assistant addressed Pandit: "For the duration."

"The duration of what?"

"Life. May I be of some aid?"

"Indeed," Pandit broke in. "What is your native tongue?"

"We have agreed to speak English here in the United States."

Pandit shot his employer a look. Plan B was in effect. He inquired: "May I ask what the ticking package addressed to you is doing in the hall?"

"To me? What ticking? What package?" The Junta Verdean advanced tentatively to the door.

"Out in the hall," Pandit called. "Here! I'll show you!" But it was Alec who advanced and with galvanic gestures put his hand on the small of the Junta Verdean's back and propelled him out the door, then slammed it and locked it. Furious pounding and shouting began.

Pandit walked slowly toward the room where Alec had once heard men sequestered. He palmed the doorknob, then turned it and abruptly pulled it to him.

Inside the room two men sat at a table, their backs to him, poring over pamphlets.

The first one had a nasal Oxbridge whine.

"I say. What cheek!" His face was obscured by large sunglasses, a black slouch hat and a copious beard. The older man was dressed in a business suit, but the top of his head was swathed in a turban, improperly wound and tied. The edge of it showed some faded lettering: *Hyde Park Hotel*.

"Begone!" he warned Pandit. "My retinue will be here momentarily. They have scimitars. Any infidel will be cut in scraps and fed to my mastiffs."

Alec peeked in.

"Pop!" he said.

8

Once the man at the door was sent away by the Wizard, and Pandit was released on his own recognizance, fifty dollars richer, Alec turned on his father: "The WEB is not your usual audience of geeks. What made you think you could get away with it? You could be arrested. I could be fired."

"I did, I wasn't, and you won't be."

"And you," Alec turned to his friend. "He's just an old con man, but you—"

"I was only trying to help," Crow protested.

"Sit down, Alec," the Wizard said. "In one week we've managed to learn more than a journalist could in a lifetime of treachery and betrayal."

"Tell him about the Garage Sale," Crow urged.

"What garage?" Alec demanded. "What sale?"

"Education." The Wizard was expansive. "Is it good or is it a service? Some would say service, like the postal, or the subways. But as for me—"

"Will you for Chrissake tell me what you have been doing in this dump for a week?"

"Fortnight, actually. We've been masking as a foreign country. An emerging nation. We sent out invitations. Nobody came. Except a handful of factotums. But we got a lot of invitations in return, Crow and I."

"There are places a correspondent can't go," Crow pointed out.

"Jail is not one of them." Alec spotted a small refrigerator and went to it. As he surmised, it was full of cheap Alabama Rhine wine, his father's favorite. He brought two bottles back with him and busied himself with the corkscrew as the Wizard bombinated.

"We set up as bewildered diplomats. Anti-colonialists. Unaligned wogs. First day, nothing happened."

"But the second—I'll have some more of that. The second," Crow amplified, "we had a visitor. White. Fat. Soft. He wanted to know if we would attend the Garage Sale."

"What kind of merch, I ask." The old man removed his headgear. "He says, 'Anything.' And he *meant* anything. Microchip heaven: watches, miniature TVs, short-wave radios."

"Is that all?"

"Well, yes." The old man was disappointed. "And some hardware, of course."

"Ah." Alec refilled his own tumbler. "What kind?"

"I don't know. It was all boxed."

"You have to order by number," said Crow. "Tell him about the catalogue."

The old man ransacked his pockets for a paper, found none, and wandered out of the room.

"Xeroxed sheet. We had to return it," said Crow. "Hundreds of choices. Radarscopes, intercontinental ballistic missiles, F-111 fighter planes, spare parts, very interesting stuff."

Alec searched his friend's face for antic signs. Except for a certain hazy quality around the eyes there was nothing to suggest he was inventing anything. Still, you could never tell. He made his living by lying to millions of people every night. He was good at it. Friends, Alec thought. Relatives. What a blessing orphans had, and solitaries.

"Where is this flea market?" he asked.

"Different places each time. They'll call us."

"And another thing, Crow—how the hell come Junta Verde is violating human rights, when there isn't any Junta Verde and there aren't any humans in it?"

"That's a little harsh, don't you think? I mean, your father and me, we're not exactly chopped liver."

The Wizard stepped back in the room. "Actually, we informed on ourselves. It's much the best way. There was a form letter. You check whatever kind of government you have: monarchy, caretaker, socialist, democracy, etc. And then you list how many political prisoners you have. If you're totalitarian you don't get any headlines unless you have"—he checked his notes—"more than fifteen thousand. If you're a democracy, five cons gets you condemned by the World Body."

"And what kind of government do you have?" Alec inquired. "I mean, in case Rand McNally calls?"

"I said we were Tory anarchists. And I told him we only had two hundred and fifty politicals. If I said none they'd think I was lying."

"My own father," Alec said. "We're all going to get arrested, you know that?"

"Nonsense! You're going to be famous after you expose us. You'll force the secretary-general to spill the whole story."

"Gruner? He never sees the press."

"He'll see you. I just now sent him a telegram. Told him one of the delegations to the World Body was fake. Said it was going to be exposed on the 7:00 news if he didn't call by noon tomorrow. Signed your name."

Alec choked on his wine.

"Gratitude is extraneous," the Wizard protested. "It's the least I could do."

It took the Heimlich Maneuver to restore air to Alec's lungs, and even then he had to be helped into the cab. He did not fully recover his wind until that evening, nor his composure until 11:55 the following morning when the phone rang.

"Hold for the secretary-general of the World Body." The excited voice had the tone of a commercial heralding a rise in compound interest.

"Halloo?"

"Mr. Secretary?"

"Ay ban Bjørn Gruner. Yü ban"—papers were shuffled and consulted—"Alec Lessing? De yürnalist?"

"Yes."

"Frum de netvürk?"

"Yes, sir."

"Yü know the identity of the bogüs delegation?"

"Well, Mr. Secretary, I—"

"Ay give yü tü minutes."

"When?"

"How süne can yü get here?"

"That's me at the door."

The secretary-general's office was located on the thirty-sixth floor of the World Body, far above the river and the city. Its thermopane windows, heavily frosted, gave an impression of eternal winter one inch away. A decorator had recently been at work, removing the furniture of the previous secretary-general, a Belgian of colonial ancestry who favored bamboo chairs, palm fronds, and the warm jungle-colored carpets of his childhood. Bjørn Gruner had a Viking distrust of heat. His rug was white, his walls pale blue. Everything else was glass or molded lucite: the desk, chairs, ashtrays, light fixtures, and sculpture: two immense ice cubes entitled *The Grimm Bros.*

Alec pretended to admire the artwork, rubbing his mouth with his hand, nodding and uttering sage, introspective grunts as he scrutinized the work. A receiver lay embedded deep in the Styrofoam base.

"Nice in here, yes?" Gruner rubbed his hands together. Steam issued from his mouth. Like the Wizard, he preferred a low thermostat. Alec realized that the frost on the windows was not an ornament; it was the real thing.

"Nice," Alec tried to agree, but his lower jaw trembled with the cold.

"Reminds me of the fjords of my yüth. Ay get yü something? Coffee?"

"Yes, coffee, fine."

Gruner asked Mrs. Ingebord to hurry with refreshment for the Secretarial guest. Moments later the prim matron passed through, bearing a silver tray with cream, sugar, and a tall glass of iced coffee. Alec's numb fingers could barely hold it.

"Now." Gruner returned to his desk. "What's dis about bogüs embassies? Yü want more ice? Ay get an icicle from de ceiling."

"No! Thanks. Mr. Secretary, this country we spoke of. It has two phony ambassadors."

"Tü? Ay know nations with fifty phony ambassadors."

"Mr. Secretary, if I name this place on the news a lot of heads are going to fall around here."

"Inclüding mine, ay suppose. Always ay hear dese threats. Yet here ay am."

Alec shrugged and began to rise.

"Still," the secretary waved him back with a gesture,

"Ay dü yü a favor. Ay lüke into de matter. Yü give me de name."

"No, Mr. Secretary."

"No? But yü said—"

"I won't *give* you the name. I'll trade it to you."

"So." Gruner's eyes narrowed. He disliked bargaining at bazaars; better to pay the list price than haggle. "Trade for what?"

"Give me Ambassador Steelhead."

"He is not mine tü give."

"Maybe not. But you could release some information about him."

"Ha. Information. Delegates keep müme about everything. Up here ay see nothing. Ay hear nothing."

Alec rose. His feet were too cold to convey sensation but he propelled himself mechanically to the sculpture. "Maybe you don't listen closely enough." He tapped the bottom of *The Grimm Bros.*

Gruner hesitated. "Yü are not quite the nincompüpe ay supposed," he conceded. The secretary-general looked straight ahead, his pale blue eyes fixed on some recollected object, an avalanche perhaps, or a half-forgotten February of his childhood.

"Ay tell yü what. Ay go out to the yon."

"The yon?"

"The men's rüme. Fife minutes ay give yü. No more."

Before Alec could reply Gruner walked briskly past him, removed an electronic device from his pocket, pressed something, and walked out. As the door hissed shut behind him, crackling sounded. Background noise issued from the sculpture, indistinctly at first, then with growing clarity:

"Always something in the way," *The Grimm Bros.* said. "Meetings, conferences, obligations."

Alec recognized the voice: the bug ran straight to Steelhead's office. There was only one speaker; obviously, the U.S. Ambassador to the WEB was having a telephone conversation. ". . . We can't afford to buy. Make sure we're outbid. Just get the price up as high as we can before we drop out. . . . Yes. A question of nice judgment." A buzzer sounded. Steelhead put his listener on hold and dealt with some papers. Rustling and the scratch of a pen sounded faintly. Dale's voice mumbled indistinctly about meetings and plenary sessions in five minutes and withdrew. Steelhead resumed: "I have to go. Call me after the Garage Sale." He hung up and made another call, this time to some under-secretary, asking for background information on the Fiji Islands. WEB business.

The door opened and *The Grimm Bros.* were abruptly silenced.

"Ay hope yü were not bored," Gruner said. He returned to his seat.

"Not at all."

"Now," Gruner no longer looked impassive; a darkness appeared behind his glacial calm, "yü talk tü me. Yü tell me about bogüs delegates."

Alec prepared to delay, to deflect, when an unlikely source reprieved him.

"Telephone call for Mr. Lessing on three." The secretary's information was conveyed by an intercom. Gruner pointed to a phone near Alec's chair. "Hold for General Wolfe."

The voice immediately boomed: "Alton?"

Alec sighed. "Yes, General."

"I imagine you're onto something. Very good. Excellent."

"Yes."

"Big stuff? Splendid."

"The biggest."

"Have you time to see me? I thought so."

"Certainly."

"When? Fine."

"Now."

Gruner's look of disappointment nourished Alec all the way to the network. The idea of eavesdropping on Steelhead was so warming that he forgot about the Arctic chill during General Wolfe's sermonets on electronic journalism.

"Watchdog of government . . . enormous responsibility to the viewer . . . accuracy in reporting . . . eyes and ears of the electorate . . . electronic newspaper . . . moral radar . . . global village . . ." The platitudes detonated around Alec as he withdrew to his private considerations. Gruner, he concluded, must be tapping Steelhead night and day.

How long had the Swede been listening to the American ambassador? Was Steelhead the only one he was tapping? What else had he heard about the Garage Sale? A man with Gruner's surveillance techniques would know all about Junta Verde by now. Alec writhed uncomfortably. He ought to warn the Wizard and Crow. But the General went on endlessly: "Policy decisions . . . highest levels of government . . ."

"I wonder if I could make a call?" his listener interrupted.

"Magnificent opportunity . . . fate of the country . . . Call? Certainly."

Wolfe indicated an extension nearby. Junta Verde was not answering. Alec shrugged and returned to his chair. The General consulted his schedule.

"When can we expect a report on Steelhead? Excellent."

"I can give you one now."

"With definite proof of his malefactions? I suppose that'll do."

"In a few days."

The General saw his correspondent out. "Very good spadework," he said. "Mrs. Wolfe has exacting standards, but she's never wrong. She knew you would be a first-class investigative reporter the second she saw your chin."

Alec kept rubbing that part of his face all the way to Sixty-second Street. At the corner, taxis honked arythmically and drivers yelled imprecations out of their windows. Pedestrians ignored red lights and worked their way around two police cars and a fire truck. The air was saturated with thick black smoke issuing from the roof of a nearby brownstone. Alec blinked through the urban fog. Breezes moved the air and he looked up again at the fire. He recognized the building now; it was the home of the Junta Verde legation. He worked his way through the crowd, but as he reached the building a cordon of police held him back. He flashed his press card.

"Already somebody in there from the network," said the sergeant.

And a moment later Boris and Pandora came down the steps, coughing. They recognized Alec. "Too late," Pandora advised him. "Nothing there to see but plaster."

Alec took hold of her shoulders. "Anybody hurt?"

"No," she said. Boris added: "Couldn't be hurt. Dead maybe, but not hurt. An explosion like that either kills you or it misses you completely. Must have been a world-class bomb." Far down the block Alec had discerned the familiar figure of the Lilliputian getting into a taxi.

Alec worked his way down Lexington Avenue, dropping quarters in phone booths, trying to reach his father. The line was always busy. He took a subway out and leaned on the bell until the door swung open and a voice yammered, "Whaddya want? You realize it's the middle of the night?"

"It's three in the afternoon for the rest of us, Titania. My father home?"

"I dunno." She let him in. "We sleep in separate bedrooms. I'm allergic."

She followed him down the hall.

Alec knocked once and opened the door. The Wizard inclined on several oversized pillows in the manner of a caliph. "Come in," he said pleasantly. "I was just watching the news. Pretty big bomb for such a little place. Makes a man feel humble."

He switched off the set. Titania closed the door and left father and son alone.

"What happened, Pop?"

"What do you mean, what happened? They blew us up. I thought the terrorists would cotton to the whole thing soon enough. They knew that we had stumbled onto the International Garage Sale. They had to knock us off. That's why I was nine miles away when it happened."

"Who did it? Who blew the place up?"

"Them. Whoever doesn't like investigative reporters."

"*You* an investigative reporter?"

"Well," the old man admitted with becoming modesty, "me and Crow. I tell you, that boy is the best acolyte I ever had. In two weeks he's learned more about chicanery than you did in a lifetime."

"Listen, Pop—"

"Not your fault; he was just born with the God-given aptitude for deceit. Crow's got so he won't even tell me his newest shell game. Something to do with an armory."

"Where is he, Pop? Where is he?"

"I left word on his service not to go to work. I had a feeling this was the day for the bomb." The Wizard looked at Alec. For the first time distress showed on the old man's face. "I thought he was with you. . . ."

Particles of mist dotted everyone's camera lenses. A series of wipers were brought out by the newspaper photographers and television cameramen. These were echoed, in miniature, by handkerchiefs used from time to time when the speakers raised a memory of special poignance. The colorless sky all but buried the sun; it was a thin white wheel the size and shape of the network logo. Everyone was moist. Clothing adhered to the skin like old bandages. The Wizard refused to attend the funeral because it smacked of religious ritual. But he appeared at the gravesite and, standing a few steps away from the large knot of mourners, removed his hat and held it briefly before his face. The gesture allowed him to pay respect to the departed as he sipped Scotch from a small, oddly curved tube secreted in the sweatband.

Laura was in the back of the group. She stood alone, nodding to an acquaintance here and there, remembered from network parties in the old days. She had been crying, but now her eyes were dry. Alec joined her and, for one moment, when he held out his hand she took it. Nothing erotic accompanied the embrace, but she made no attempt to pull away and when he looked at her, her gaze was steady. She managed a brief smile and then the tears returned.

"We are assembled here to pay tribute to a man of talent and great"—the General blinked to the cameras and addressed three microphones—"resources. He was a man always in search of something and someone new. A man," he added ambiguously, "who gave new meaning to the word integrity."

Grambling waited for his chief to finish, then added his own observations about the deceased. Alec was afraid the news editor might remind viewers of Crow's long list of on-the-air bloopers: the time he asked viewers to stay tuned for a BBC production of "Rictoria Vagina," how he had described the chairman of the Olympic committee as "Pimp and Circumstance." But Grambling decided to re-tell a long, colorless anecdote about the responsibility of the electronic journalist.

The electronic journalist. The term had always made Alec uncomfortable; it reminded him of his father's closeup effects: the Invisible Coin, the Steaming Cowflop, the Electronic Journalist. It was not difficult for Alec to spot his colleagues at the gravesite. The others, the curious, gawking viewers, Crow's family of pale dark-haired cousins, shifted uneasily from foot to foot, slightly bent, uncomfortable, unsure of how to display or hide sorrow. Even the newspaper reporters were abashed in the presence of mourning. But the television men and women had long practice at the art of display. Their lives were dedicated to the eradication of privacy in all its forms. Politicians would be trained to walk along the beach in what the network would describe as "solitude": one man treading sand, with camera and sound teams keeping pace on the dunes. Women whose children had been kidnapped from a day care center would be interviewed in the back of a police car, the microphone thrust near their teeth; separating couples would be ambushed at their apartment houses or at stage entrances: PIRK, the public's inalienable right to know. The electronic journalists had seen it all. They stood now, looking at the speaker or at the closed coffin or at the army of erect memorial stones, and they wore their solemnity with ease, like umbrellas. Only their eyes roved, checking the crowd for celebrities who might be questioned afterward, in order to steal an extra step on a rival for the better quote, the more revealing footage.

Grambling finished and returned to the General's side.

The last speaker approached the little platform. She was an old arthritic Irishwoman in black linen, and she spoke in a high, quavering tone about the deceased. "A grand, sympathetic soul," she said. "He brought me back from ruin. Up on Third Avenue I was, sworn never to be sober till Belfast and Dublin had reunited. But he taught me that first I would have to reunite the separate parts of my eternal soul. . . ." Alec looked at her casually, then with increasing scrutiny. The white hair was a wig, of that he was sure. And the face—surely makeup was responsible for many of those creases. And the accent was a bit off-tone. The eyes were familiar. Who was she? And then he knew. And so did Laura. Behind the tears they saw a merry, malicious glint. The bag lady was Linda the horsewoman, Linda née Drysdale, Crow's ex-wife. Crow had said something about renewing a business relationship with her. And now here she was, doing the act she had been scheduled for on the Good News portion of the show, before the explosion.

No wonder the Wizard, in the back row behind the civilians, was uncertain of whether to laugh or weep. To the end, even at his own funeral, Crow was still conning the audience. The Wizard had lost his spiritual son.

A group of correspondents and network executives would be gathering at the Narcissus now, awaiting the General's post-funeral pronunciamentos on television and life. Alec knew that his absence would be noted. Let them talk; it no longer mattered. Laura was due at her publisher's; he returned to his lonely, meaningless patrol at the WEB. The delegates' lounge was open. He isolated himself at a rear table to read his book and devise his next move. There would be very little time; the Lilliputian had learned about the false embassy. He might have been the one who

torched it. There was no proof, of course, and even if Alec
had fingerprints and photographs, the terrorists had diplomatic immunity. Halifax would be at home in the World
Body; hypocrisy was his meat.

In a corrupt age, the putting of the world in order would
breed confusion.

"These are not being used?"
Alec looked up. The broad flat face of the Soviet delegate smiled down. His little eyes displayed a porcine interest in the bowl of crackers neglected at Alec's table, and the
nostrils of his snout were wide with anticipation.
"All yours."
Yuri Andilov took the gesture for an invitation. He sat
down importantly. The chair cushion hissed. He placed a
corner of the cracker dish on his lower lip and tilted the
contents into his mouth. A package, hastily gift-wrapped,
was lowered to the table as he munched noisily. "I was
going to leave this in the press room. Then I saw you. Fate.
Here."
"Thank you."
"Open."
Numbly, Alec plucked at the string.
"I used to watch constantly your colleague on TV,"
Andilov went on. "I like the sports. Especially golf. All
those sticks and no one permitted to talk during the hit-
ting."
Alec removed the outer layers and peeked in the box.
"A toaster. In the U.S. banks give these when you open
an account. We give when you close out."
Alec put the cover back on.
"If you don't like you could exchange. It comes from
Two Guys just off the Woodbridge cloverleaf."

"No, it's fine. I'll give it to his family. Very kind."

"Nothing. Thank you for the crackers." And he was gone. Alec looked for a waiter, but before he could call, Mr. Fong, from the People's Republic of China, appeared.

"You will forgive me, I hope." He introduced himself. "The occasion is very melancholy."

"Yes."

"A minuscule condolence." He remained standing even when Alec indicated the chair, and placed his package on the table next to the toaster. "Please accept."

"Of course."

Mr. Fong opened this one himself. An oven toaster gleamed in the shredded newspaper. He regarded the present from the Soviet Union with disdain. "Typical," he said. "Ours holds twice as much. Even grills cheese. Yet pennies per day to operate."

Mr. Fong was replaced by a small delegation from the Organization of African States. They presented a clock radio.

"If you should, so to speak, open an account with us," they offered, "we have other compelling premiums."

So did the uncommitted bloc; the European Economic Community, the Benelux nations, the nonaligned countries. Gifts piled up on the table: wristwatch alarms, a fifteen-piece set of Ginsu carving knives, a Pac-Man television game; a cordless telephone, smoke detectors. The packages, arranged in a pyramid, obscured Alec until all that could be seen was his hand, shaken in condolence by delegate after delegate.

He could no longer see those who presented the gifts, nor hear them over the crackling of paper. When the last hand was extended he shook it automatically before he noticed that it lacked professional sinew. He tried to rise.

"Don't bother," she said, and pushing aside some donations, Laura sat on the edge of a box marked Very Old

Very Special Japanese Scotch Whiskey.

"I thought you had a meeting."

She moved more of the gifts until Alec's face appeared.

"I just didn't want to talk contracts. Not now, not today."

"What do you want to talk about?"

"I don't know." She looked away. "Could we get out of here?"

"Where would you like to go?"

"Isn't this where I ask: 'My place or yours?' "

"We can go to a neutral corner if you want."

"That would be best."

"If you can stand it," Alec said, "I think I know where we ought to be."

Crow's apartment was not her ideal, but once she was there Laura could think of no place more appropriate. Someone had left the lights on, probably relatives searching for memorabilia, a souvenir of the departed. All the senses were reminded of Crow: pictures of him with the staff, players, and management of the Mets; the still-pervasive aroma of Vitalis, Ben-Gay, and garlic; his voice and gestures preserved on a video disc; the refrigerator stacked with Czech Pilsener Urquel, his favorite; and throughout, end tables covered with small black representations of the American Crow, his trademark on the 6:00 sportscast and on the new Good News portion. Who would sit in his place? Alec wondered. It was a little after six, and he turned on the set.

"Can't you forget your job for one night?" Laura began and then she understood. Alec was still saying good-bye.

They sat on the couch, Alec with a green bottle of Urquel in hand, Laura with a glass of water softly clinking its ice cubes. They watched themselves at the graveyard as the General's voice droned over them. Dean Steed recited the requisite valedictory to Crow just before the commercial break. When he came back he introduced the newest member of the 6:00 team. "Good evening, Pandora Skutch," she began, "this is, ladies and gentlemen . . . ." That was only the start. By the conclusion she had introduced a former gang leader as a boy who "farted stights" and who had not reformed until he had "gowned Fod."

"Who *is* she?" Laura wondered.

"Camera crew," Alec said. "She filled three quotas: Female, Balto-Slavik, Under Five Feet."

"Don't forget Tongue-tied. And Overweight. That's five quotas."

"She's not overweight. She's just a little topheavy."

"How heavy would you say, about a pound? Or do they go by kilos?"

"Laura, I hardly know her. And even if I did—"

"Sorry."

"I'm not. I'm glad you're not indifferent. Neither am I. It's difficult, sharing a child and not a life."

"Lots of people do it."

"More every year."

"Maybe they know something we don't." He snapped off the set. Dean Steed wobbled, slanted, and turned into an electronic dot before slithering into the black glass.

"Is Azie all right? I tried to get her the other night."

"We were out at the theater. She wanted to see *Oh! Calcutta!*"

"Laura, she's ten goddam years old."

"This is the marionette version. They cleaned it up. There's nothing in it but dancing. You ever seen a nude puppet?"

"No."

"Well, there's nothing provocative. It doesn't even jiggle."

"Sounds like some of my dates."

Laura smiled at him. "You still looking?"

"No time. You?"

Laura made no reply. She was looking through a stack of unopened mail: sports magazines, catalogues of out-of-print erotica, letters addressed to Occupant and announcing on the outside You May Already Be A Winner, and an unstamped, sealed letter to Alec Lessing.

"There's something here for you." Laura handed it to him. "Crow's handwriting. Go ahead, open it."

Alec hesitated: he was not a believer in voices from the grave. The envelope contained no message except for the legend "Garage Sale" written in the margin of a Polaroid. It showed the front of a redstone structure on the Upper East Side, squatting belligerently between two maximum-security condominiums. The letters over the wide oak doors read "29th Division Armory."

"Why are you looking like that?" Laura put her hand on Alec's cheek.

Crow's message was clear now. What was not clear was how much Alec should tell Laura. He hesitated, then he said, "You know, I never changed my will. You might as well know what I died for." And he told her everything he had seen and learned and guessed about the WEB.

When he finished, she said, "You won't die. You're going to scoop the world and you're going to be on all the talk shows."

"Nobody will go near me after this. Everybody believes in the WEB. The last thing anybody wants is the truth."

"The General wants it."

"We'll see." He picked up the phone and dialed the chief officer. The secretary kept him on hold for five minutes, but eventually the familiar voice boomed out: "Alben?"

"Yes, General?"

"You have news? Splendid."

"I think so, General. I may have the goods on—"

"—no names. We may be t-a-p-p-e-d."

"I need some help, General."

"What sort? Hidden cameras, mikes, that sort of thing?"

"Yes. I can't take a crew with me on this."

"Report to Studio 12. They'll take care of everything. Ask for the Claw. Tell him Groucho sent you."

"Groucho?"

"My code name. Yours is Gudgeon." He spelled it. "You're not to go through the office. Report directly to me. Got that? Splendid."

Alec said, "Yes, General," but by that time he was talking to a dial tone.

"Is there anything I can do?" Laura prepared to leave.

He put his hand on her shoulder and kissed her hair. She smelled of memories.

"Alec, don't," she told him.

"OK," he said, but he did not release her. She said "Don't" once more but when he put his hand on the top of her blouse she said nothing and when he kissed her, her mouth was open.

"You suppose he knows?" she asked later, moving away in Crow's bed.

"I think so. I think that's why we did it."

"To show we're still alive?"

"Yes."

"A simple declaration would have done."

"That was a simple declaration."

"Nothing we do is simple, Alec. Now you've disturbed my heart, and I've disturbed yours. And for what?"

"For an hour."

"Thank you very much."

"For ourselves. For old times. Come on, Laura. It wasn't so awful."

"No," she said. "That's the trouble."

9

Huckabee and Trafe insisted on a closed set. No out-
siders. The emir insisted on a live audience of his choosing,
and a group of his close personal advisers, including Alec.
Huckabee and Trafe invoked the power of their union, the
Writers Guild of America, their personal integrities, and
most sacred of all, the name of their agent. They banged
their fists on tables, shouted into phones, and rent the air
with howls and recriminations.

Twenty-four hours later, seventy-two of the emir's
onlookers watched Hamid and his friend descend from
their camels against a lurid backdrop of spray-painted sand
and sunset. Hamid indicated his tent. "Last week," he said,
"I told my mothair-een-law, 'My 'ouse is your 'ouse.' So she
sold it."

He opened the tent flap. "My wife. Can she talk! Last
wik we went to Assyria. When we got 'ome 'er tongue was
sunburned . . . She went to the astrologer for a beauty
treatment. 'E give her a mud pack. For two days she looked
terrifique. Then the mud fell off." He called out: "Baclava,
I'm 'ome!"

A large houri appeared, smirking through her veil.

"I didn't know what 'appiness was until I got married," Hamid declared. "And then it was too late. Actually,
the first part of our marriage was very 'appy. But on the
way back from the ceremony . . ."

Laughter exploded from the audience seated on

benches alongside the set of cardboard pyramids and a sphinx. All of them were obviously recruited from the emir's staff or from friendly embassies, and the amanuenses and underlings never failed to produce bursts of mirth when Daladan raised the card indicating HILARITY. He held similar posters in various tongues ordering YOCKS, TITTERS, BOFFOS, and APPLAUSE.

"So much better than tinned laughter," Hamid Daladan said. "Canned," Huckabee grumbled. "Like canned ham."

The emir grumbled. "I do not 'scarf' ham," he reminded the gagwriter and tilted his canvas chair to the left. He whispered to Alec: "The blending of two cultures is never simple. But it is always worthwhile."

Alec nodded, gratified. Every scene was more ghastly than the one before.

The emir stirred himself noisily.

"I wish to hear the message instead of mere 'yocks.' "

"Certainly, certainly, Your Majesty," replied Trafe.

"Roll 'em," said Huckabee.

The cast went back to work.

"Have a tough day at the pyramid?" Hamid's mate inquired.

"I'll say."

"Well, it hasn't been so easy here at the oasis. The baby's been terrible all day."

Hamid turned to the camera. "Just like 'is fathair. When I was born I was so ugly the doctor slapped my mothair."

His friend seated himself on the floor and groaned. "I wish we had something besides these stupid camels."

"Me, too," Hamid agreed. "But that's what 'appens when superpowers in Europe and the new world control the wealth of the planettes, robbing the deprived nations of badly needed resources. But wait! Our turn shall come, and the great Satans of the West shall be brought to their collective knees."

Gales of merriment issued from the audience. Distressed, the emir turned his attention to the card. Instead of APPLAUSE, Hamid, that bungler, was holding aloft the poster reading LAUGHTER.

"Your name?"

"Gudgeon," Alec told him. He reminded himself to look up the word some time. It sounded familiar.

"You realize, Gudgeon, that this place does not exist —that if you ever mention it to anyone, I and all the others will deny everything. And that in any case, no one will lift a finger to help you."

"Yes."

"And that this equipment is all stolen—every bit of it. You could go to prison if you're caught."

"Worth it."

The bent old artificer shook his narrow head.

"Very well. This jacket has a camera in the right shoulder pad. This tape recorder fits in your sleeve."

"What does the magnet do?"

"The one in the ace bandage on your knee? Jams tracking instruments, throws off digital clocks, things of that sort. General mischief-maker. Want a gun?"

"No thanks."

"How about a knife that folds into a coin?"

"No."

"Curare-tipped scissors? Sleeping potions in the shape of buttons? You can dissolve them in coffee. I have a special on sunglasses that fold into a slingshot. You can fire anthrax pellets."

Alec wanted none of them. Mr. Claw of Quaker Novelties to the Trade could not disguise his disappointment.

"A great pity," he said with an accent overlaid like a wall with the notices of past events and other cities. "Other gentlemen are more adventurous. I do better in Libya, Vienna, Ulster, Africa. See here: Orders for nine gross of these. And these. I go back there next week. Overseas they really appreciate an artist."

Grambling was too furious to speak. He kept pointing at Alec, then at the television monitor in back of his desk, then at an antique globe of the world as it appeared in 1300. As the blood gathered in his temples and cheeks he choked out a few words.

"You . . . went . . . to the General . . . over . . . my . . . head. You asked . . . for special . . . equipment . . . I'll . . . have . . . your ass . . . for . . . this."

"I assure you—" Alec began.

"You ever hear of the chain of command?"

"Yes." Alec wondered how soon he could decently leave. Grambling would not dare to fire him: not now. Until the exposure of Steelhead, Alec was immune. General's orders. "Yes, I know what the chain of command is. It's what keeps originality out of the 7:00 news."

Grambling took a large breath and let half of it out. He walked over to his Tunturi Exercycle and slowly worked the pedals, deflecting the symptoms of stress, just as the medical department advised.

"You think the General can protect you forever?"

"After this story breaks I won't need protection. After that—"

"After that . . ." Grambling pumped the bicycle with increasing speed. "After that . . ." He pondered the globe, mumbling of news bureaus where he might send this insubordinate, bureaus beyond the sun, places that could make the WEB seem an Eden. The pedals blurred with activity. Alec started to steal out quietly as Grambling closed his eyes. When Alec reached the door the cyclist growled, between breaths, "Whatever the hell you're doing, you're still the WEB correspondent until I tell you different, spy stuff or no spy stuff. You got that?"

"Of course."

"Tomorrow morning some babe about 106 years old, just came back from the jungle, she's going to give a speech. At the WEB. She's calling on every goddam woman to go on general strike for a day to protest war. She says, get this —" He procured a folded Xeroxed sheet from his shirt pocket. He read: "For too long man has made war on man. The arms race is nothing but men saying to other men, 'Mine's bigger than yours.' "

He looked up and said to Alec, "I don't have to tell you what she wants to have removed. All this happened while you were crapping around at the WEB. Go find this geriatric bimbo. Her name is on here."

"I think I can locate her," Alec assured him. "And I already know her name. She's my mother."

But he could not locate her. On Tuesday morning the clock radio interrupted Scarlatti to blurt bulletins about the collapse of civil law in Syria and Northern Ireland. Gibraltar had been invaded: All twenty-nine apes had been taken prisoner and given Spanish names. Britain, Canada, New Zealand, and Australia were sending submarines to the Straits. The Fiji Islands of Viti Levu, Ngau, and Koro announced that they had joined the nuclear club after the successful test of a device in Melanesia. All Asians were expelled from two Central African states; the Third World international conference on torture endorsed it during a three-day conference in Madrid; Iran banished any device made in the twentieth century from its borders, with the exception of radar and electric cattle prods.

In Eastern Europe, Soviet workers began constructing a tower from which canisters of tear gas could be dropped on agitators. Mines were discovered floating in the Panama Canal. Callers from Libya, Zaire, Cyprus, all claimed credit for the devices. A rocket of unknown origin landed in the Gobi Desert. As Mongols approached it on camel it exploded, charring the contents beyond recognition, although one of the Mongols reported that he had heard a Chinese voice croaking signals just before the detonation. Satellite photographs confirmed that a wall, much like the one in Berlin, was under construction on the borders between South Africa and Zimbabwe. Full-page advertisements bloomed on the back page of the *Morning Paper* decrying war and promoting peace as if those terms had never before been printed. The notices were endorsed by actresses, rabbis, professors, a maverick priest who signed petitions in favor of abortion on demand, congressmen and women, scientists, feminists, and two Broadway producers. At the lower right corner of the page was a coupon listing a place to send money so that more ads could be printed.

The World Body awoke, twitching. Titular and political leaders flew in to the city demanding to be heard. Ambassador Steelhead clicked off Gomer Pyle and dubbed these men and women Warheads, a sobriquet repeated in the great black headlines of the *Afternoon Paper*. After inquiries from the White House and several long-distance calls, the ambassador revised his estimate.

Steelhead Misspeaks Himself Again," said the story in the *Morning Paper* the next day. "Meant Meatheads." As the day drew on Meat became Fat, then Pot, Acid, and, in the end, mere Hotheads. Again the administration was forced, for the twenty-first time, to defend its ambassador to the World Body, praising him in a terse, two-paragraph statement as a "dedicated worker for human rights with an unblemished record of public service."

"Last time they said 'unparalleled' worker for human rights," Hackett noted. "This time only 'dedicated.' Beginning of the end, Squire."

Alec agreed. Saturday would be the best, perhaps the last time to act.

He prepared his equipment and his papers. The last will and testament, leaving everything to Azie in the event of catastrophe, was in order. The scraps of evidence and overheard conversation were spoken into his Panasonic tape recorder, then the tape was addressed to the Wizard and mailed. There was nothing to do but wait for interruptions.

The first occurred on Thursday morning.

"Alec?"

"Pop?"

"Catastrophe!"

"War?"

"Worse."

"Money?"

"Worse."

"Disease?"

"Worse."

"Famine?"

"Worse."

"Mom?"

"Exactly."

"Where?"

"WEB."

"Ah."

"Tomorrow."

"Morning?"

"Nine."

"Thanks."

"Sorry."

In that word, the Wizard, hanging up with a sigh, conveyed the weight of four and a half decades of married life, most of them adulterous, all marked by skirmishes and sometimes bloodletting battles. Yet Alec knew that his father was nostalgic for times when the Junoesque brunette, in rented spangled tights, bounced for the delectation of the yokels while the Wizard, dressed in the only unpatched garments he owned, claw-hammer coat and striped formal trousers, flourished pigeons from his cummerbund and shook dollar bills from an empty ice-water pitcher. So it was not only curiosity that brought Josiah Lessing to the galleries the following morning, nor the wish to see his wife make an idiot of herself with her loud, omnipresent red hat and her vast flower-print dress straining at its seams. From across the room Alec watched the Wizard's face crinkle when he found the auditorium full of the curious and the press. As people claimed their seats the old man spotted his son, his ex-daughter-in-law, and their daughter Azie. The audience recognized him immediately, not because of his relation to the advertised speaker but because of his TV appearances. "The Wizard," he heard them buzz behind him, and, flourishing the Straw Hat that Leaks and the Personal Vibrator With a Memory, he entertained all those around him, intermittently signing autographs even when he had not been asked.

Alec watched his father bring forth a bouquet made of toilet paper. "That's his secret," he said to Laura. "An absolute lack of taste."

She watched their daughter standing near the Wizard, enchanted. "All she talked about this morning was seeing Grandma and Grandpa. Kids like everything to be just the way it was. They're the real conservatives. It's the grown-ups that want changes."

Alec slid his seat down beside her. He indicated the Wizard. "How do you explain him? He wants the same thing all the time: applause."

"That's not a grownup," she said. A cascade of confetti rained down on those near the old magician. Azie, who had sought him out, planted a kiss on his cheek. He autographed her hand with a ballpoint pen before he recognized his granddaughter, then shooed her away as a gavel pounded at the rostrum. She made her way back to her parents and sat noisily between them just as the meeting was brought to order.

The chairperson, a wiry California beautician with the cold glower of a water-moccasin, acknowledged the presence of the press and honored guests, and gave a brief biography of the speaker. Lenore Lessing had left a career in show business as a sex object to become a rallying point for interhemispherical feminism. Wife, mother, explorer, ethnologist, mutant, she was known only to a few at first. But as her consciousness rose, her trips south covered more and more mileage until at last, after the Carolinas, Mexico, and Panama, she landed near the leafy Amazon, in search of the original feminists: warriors, it was said, who cultivated enormous Venus flytraps capable of consuming a man down to his shoelaces. Alas, she was unable to find even a single member of the tribe. At first, she thought they might be legendary after all, fantasies of a *belle idéal.* But no, she came to realize. They were extinct, annihilated by savage males with spears.

And what were spears, really? Everyone knew. "Today, all over this beleaguered globe," she declared, "in every member nation of the World Body, men are savaging women with their fleshly spears. And not only fleshly. From the claim of 'Mine's bigger than yours' come the symbols of—yes, let us dissemble no longer my friends, listeners, ladies and others—genital rivalry. After the shlong, the spear, after the spear, the sword, the bullet, the cannon, the rocket. Penis to the moon, phalluses waiting in submarines and silos. No longer toys, no longer mere tools of rape. The world is much too hazardous for these male things." Anthony, her newly adopted son, stood fidgeting in the wings, lightly picking the pocket of an arthritic custodian.

The only way out, Lenore warned her listeners, was to "discard weapons as we know them, to throw away or abandon all the missiles, the smart bombs, the intercontinental organs." Her voice rose. "I'm not naive, I know the impossibility of total disarmament. Each nation needs protection from its neighbors. I ask only that the imagery of the male give way to that of the more numerous and longer-lived sex. Vaginal symbols are what are needed in these crucial times. Traps. Pits, Snares. Meshes and toils. Nets."

Someone opened doors in the rear of the auditorium. Journalists looked in and hurried on. Bigger news was taking place down the hall. Lenore continued, but she was losing her audience. The faithful stayed, holding the emblem of their creed: fishnets with bright red handles. They applauded their leader when she spoke of a world of Hav-a-Hart traps in which soldiers would be humanely captured in wire mesh devices, like field mice, then disarmed and released in meadows. But cheers grew pale as the audience thinned out. They were on their way to larger rallies with more formidable names. The new session of the World Body had begun.

Alec worked his way to the back and peered out. The President of the United States had arrived; behind him came the heads of African, European, and Asian states. Dignitaries and politicians of every sort entered. Back in Paris and London Alec had interviewed most of them:

superannuated ministers of state, young dictators with mad, glistening eyes and faces of incalculable depravity; pompous admirals of fleets containing one battleship and twelve freighters of dubious registration; regal pretenders to thrones unfilled since the Russian Revolution; elected representatives, hereditary chieftains, autarchs who had murdered their way to the top. All were here accompanied by bodyguards. All were enjoying or ignoring the questions of the suddenly awakened press. All were delighting in the privilege of diplomatic immunity by double-parking their cars in front of churches, department stores, and intersections, kiting checks, and neglecting to pay restaurant bills.

Alec returned to his seat, waiting for his mother to finish. But she showed no signs of winding up or down. The lights dimmed and Lenore showed slides of her expedition along the Amazon. Alligators appeared, sometimes upside down. Then tribeswomen and dugout canoes, trading posts, grinning indecipherable masks, then clearings and little villages, and finally strange, gleaming cities with rectangular buildings lining streets that went nowhere at all, hacked out of the jungle, paved and curbed, alive with taxis and shoppers with European haircuts and sunglasses, attempting to appear as young as diet and surgery would allow. As Lenore narrated, Anthony moved through the aisles, snuggling against one or another of the watchers as he went through her purse or satchel.

"I've got to cover the arrivals," Alec whispered.

"Coward," Laura hissed.

"Come with me."

"No, we'll wait. Let Azie see Grandma up close."

"Grandma looks better from a distance," Alec said. "About two furlongs distance." But he stayed.

The last slide faded and the lights snapped on, revealing an almost empty house. Only a few of the loyalists had remained. Anthony lay on the stage floor, snuffling; there were no more sheep to fleece. Azie and Laura approached, cautiously stepping over him.

Lenore turned to them.

"Ah," she said. "The nuclear family. Come. Let me introduce you. Anthony, stop playing with that and put your pants on this instant. Say hello to your relatives."

She introduced them. Anthony stuck out his hand and his tongue. He went to Alec and allowed himself to be picked up from the ground. But Alec, an old observer of carnival dips, cannons, and other pickpockets, grabbed his half-brother's hand at the wrist so tightly that the dreadful child ululated in his native tongue: *"Tonga remadu kilimonda!"*

"He says you are the product of a blue ape's abortion," confided a voice below Alec. It was Pandit. "My goodness! One has not heard that language in many years."

Alec released Anthony. The boy retreated, yowling.

"A great blessing when a family can be together." Pandit patted Anthony on the head and, with the hand-eye coordination that had made him a Ping-Pong champion in his native country, swiftly withdrew his fingers before the boy could bite them. Anthony's teeth clicked on the air.

Alec introduced Pandit to his mother.

"Yes," he said. "I could hear much of your speech. Very fine. Especially the part about legs. The leg, you know, is the best part of—"

"But I said nothing about legs."

"No? Ah well, it was another speech then. One hears so many. Everyone is talking at the same time in the hall: Disarmament, West, East, Third World, New World, Old World, rockets, gross national product, peacekeeping forces, legs, it is hard to keep track. Perhaps it was merely two journalists talking."

Lenore turned away to her lieutenant, a large woman with a whiskey contralto. "Journalists remind me," she

said; "arrange a press conference for five. I'm going to call
the national strike." She suddenly turned to Alec. "Hell,"
she said, "I forgot. You're a journalist. You wouldn't break
this, would you? You wouldn't sell out your mother?"
Alec was silent, pondering.
"Of course he wouldn't." The Wizard advanced toward his wife, ready to dispense a bear hug. She shrank
back adroitly. "Wonderful to see you. Wonderful," he
boomed. "And this must be Anthony." He extended his
hand. Anthony took it, intending to convey it to his sharp
little teeth. But the Wizard had secreted an electronic
buzzer in his palm. Anthony shrieked and backed away.
More imprecations followed.
"A rich vocabulary," said Pandit. "He should be working here at the World Body."
The Wizard turned to his wife. "What say we all meet
at your hotel later, discuss old times? I want to hear about
your trip. Did you bring any slides? I fell asleep earlier. It's
these antihistamines." He produced a little pillbox, but
Lenore had turned away furiously and started to convey
Anthony and her staff into the wings.
The Wizard turned to Alec sadly. "She's right. You
can't sell out your own mother." He brightened. "But I
can." And he went to call in the news about the Women's
General Strike.
Pandit said, "I'm very glad to be running into you,
Alec. I have a message." He consulted a wrinkled envelope.
"I cannot make out the name. He said to tell you that the
Garage Sale is noon, one day earlier. At the same place."
"Who told you that?"
"The telephone. He was asking for a translator. Then
he asked me if I knew a Mr. Lessing. I said yes. Then he
said about the sale. So many calls today. Perhaps I wrote
the name."
He showed his message pad to Alec. "I wrote in Urdu.
But I was thinking in Czech. And he was speaking in En-

glish, I think. Perhaps Swedish. Impossible to say now."

Alec thanked him and took his wife and child from the madhouse. They decided to go back to Laura's. Through the revolving door at the front entrance they went, past the picketers calling for unilateral disarmament. Before Pandit deciphered his handwriting, they were gone.

"I have the signature now!" The translator held the pad aloft and read, "Gregory Ellenbogen. The real Gregory Ellenbogen." No one paid the slightest attention to him. He was shouting in Swahili.

10

Cable offered Alec twenty-seven channels, and he tried them all, whirling the dial like a croupier. Except for the commercials, there was no relief. On channel K, paratroopers landed gently, like milkweed seeds, and ran over the parched Saudi desert. On the network, the Tokyo airlift began: tanks and tanks of oxygen were released into the city's contaminated atmosphere, allowing its citizens to breathe once again without masks. Alec dialed on. Haiti and Cuba continued to mine each other's harbors, but currents kept sweeping the devices far from their intended places: one was responsible for the sinking of a whaler off Denmark. A declaration of war, the first between Scandinavian and Caribbean countries, was said to be only hours away. Chad tested a small nuclear device on an unpopulated island in the São Tomé chain. The border skirmishes between Chile and Argentina widened. No one had yet explained what Brazilian mercenaries were doing with Russian MIGs, Austrian photographic equipment, French air-to-air missiles, and Japanese radar when they violated Israeli air space and were pursued and downed in the Greek islands.

Hundreds of thousands of scientists gathered in St. James's Park to protest . . .

"Is this the end of the world?" Azie asked. She and Shawna were abstractedly consuming frozen yogurts and sampling the news. The question was asked out of curiosity, not concern.

"I don't think so. When it's the end there's supposed to be trumpets."

Alec looked at them, unfinished pink creatures, restive little souls in the official uniform of the private school at rest: jeans, Indian blouses, and Tretorns with floral-print laces, hair washed the night before, now a gathering of wild tendrils reaching for the light in a city that was notorious for stealing childhood from children. Would they have a chance to be women? Or *was* this some kind of finish to civilization?

"I haf to go," Shawna said, crunching the last shards of cone. "Six A.M. I'm in a commercial for anti-nuke deodorant. It's called *Disarmament.*" For Alec's benefit she explained further: "People sweat a lot at rallies." And at the door: "They were going to call it *Disunderarmament.* But it sounded tacky."

"Yes, I can see that." Alec stepped out into the hall. "You want me to find a cab?"

"No, there's a chariot downstairs."

And so there was. As Alec and Azie watched from the window, Shawna mounted a golden vehicle pulled by two chestnut geldings and driven by a human male equivalent in a toga. On the side of the chariot stenciled letters read: "Shawna Cosmetics—Ahead of the Future, Aware of the Past."

Azie waved until the horses clopped around the corner and Shawna disappeared.

"How do you stay ahead of the future?" Alec asked his daughter. "It's like being in front of your nose."

"It's just hype," she reminded him.

As she gathered her notebook, Alec wondered if there were any entries in there about him; how a girl assayed her father so often predicted the way she would conduct herself with men. Would she grow into one of those sullen women with holistic therapies and quick, unpredictable squalls? Or would she run shy of men: all glances and ironic deflections, a loner or a joiner of groups where sex became politics and there were only sisters and the enemy? He tried to imagine a series of women, but he saw only a child; he would always look at her and see a child, he thought— a parent's disease. He doubted whether he would have the privilege, the indulgence, of watching her grow. There was every reason to believe that he would end like poor Crow. Except that, with luck, he would have his story on the air before he went.

"Azie," he began, "if for some reason—"

The phone interrupted him.

General Wolfe's secretary asked him to hold, but the General got on immediately.

"You prepared? I assumed so."

"All ready."

"Equipment in good shape? That's fine."

"Yes."

"Odd, changing the schedule like that. Almost as if they knew we were up to something. You didn't say anything to anyone? I didn't think so."

"Of course not. Are you the one that called me, General?"

"Eight o'clock then. Tonight. Good luck, Alex." The last phrase was said with one of the General's British flight-squadron intonations, learned from years of watching his network's afternoon revivals of J. Arthur Rank movies. A brief, flashing passage from one of those films played in some dark wrinkle of Alec's brain and disappeared. He felt a chill.

"I should go?" Azie said. It was meant as a statement, but the last syllable rose and produced a question.

"Yes, I think maybe . . . Azie . . ."

But she had collected her books and drawing pad. He found no way to unburden his heart and they took a cab down to Laura's, chatting emptily about a trip to the planetarium.

"There's a show: The Last Day on the Earth," Azie said. A show, Alec thought. That was the way it would probably end: advertised in the theater listings, with special rates for groups.

"How do you think the world will end?"

"I don't know," Alec replied absently. "Maybe it's already ended."

But Azie was no longer listening. The taxi had stopped for a red light and she stared out the window at a man, bare to the waist, with a python coiled generously around his neck. A group circled him.

"There's a snake like that in our neighborhood," Azie observed. "Different man, though."

The python impudently flicked its tongue at them as they moved on.

Alec hoped that Laura was home. But she had left a note for Azie on the kitchen table: *Out shopping, back by 5.* He could not afford to wait. He kissed his daughter and stared at her a long while, fixing her in his mind.

Alec had been in his apartment less than fifteen minutes when a staccato knock began at the metal front door. He looked through the tiny glass peephole. A round-faced, pleasant man in livery stood impatiently, shifting his considerable bulk.

"I'm from the network," the man bellowed. "The General's personal chauffeur. Brogan. I drove you Armed Forces Day."

"So you did," Alec agreed, and opened the door.

"The General wants me to take you personal."

"You know the address?"

"Yeah."

"I'm not ready yet."

"I'll wait. You got anything to drink?"

Alec examined the refrigerator.

"A six-pack of Ballantine ale."

"That'll do." Brogan annihilated all six cans while Alec dressed and secreted his cameras and microphones. On the way to the Garage Sale, Brogan stopped off at a Gristede's for another six-pack. He drained a can as he drove, humming some bars from "Paper Moon."

Old forebodings advanced from their burrows, then retreated at the noise of the driver who alternately sang, expelled air, and rustled paper. As he pulled up before the school, Brogan handed Alec a small plastic card.

"From the General," he said. "Stick it in your wallet."

Alec read the card. Barely legible Greek identified the visitor as an assistant delegate from the Isle of Procrustes. Alec's photograph, heat-sealed in the upper right corner, had been taken from a publicity shot in Antwerp after an economics conference. The unlined face smiled out at an older, sadder self.

Brogan let him out at the armory. Alec walked up the steps behind two bearded and mustachioed men talking in animated Spanish. At his back were five men of various origins speaking heavily-accented French. They all had identical beards and mustaches. Alec's credentials were checked twice by guards in gray uniforms before he could be led to a large echoing room with high ceilings and mullioned windows. A long red banner was stretched from wall to wall, and the blue letters on it read *Blessed are the Peacekeepers*. The long oak floorboards, streaked with the rubber of uncounted boots, were visible only in small islands, between the herds and gatherings of shoppers examining vast displays of merchandise.

"Now *that* is what Ah call fair."

The voice seemed to echo another time, another arena. The omnipresent resin smile and rumpled suit suggested an air of genial informality while the right hand tightened on a shopper's arm.

"Tell you what," the speaker promised. "I'll throw in the grenades gratis."

His customer was an undersized tanned officer who licked his lips at the hardware assembled on a white metal table, as if the small arms were hors d'oeuvres. Except for the mustache and goatee, Alec mused, the salesman might be Senator Bland. He had not seen the senator since the night of his return to the states; he might easily be mistaken. Besides, why would a high official involve himself in the International Garage Sale? The crowd pushed on.

Nearby, two heat-seeking missiles pointed upward, painted flesh-color.

Moving from group to group, straining for phrases in English or French, Alec found the reverse side of the World Body. Here, an entrepreneur from White Africa, which constitutionally forbade communism, was doing a brisk trade in shotguns with two Czech salesmen. Israelis peddled automatic rifles to Iraquis through a third party of unidentified origin, a long, narrow man dressed in rumpled tan poplin, reminiscent of a wine bottle in a paper bag. When they were not checking the crowd, security guards looked up at convex mirrors normally used by department stores to spot shoplifters. They showed images of turbaned, bearded negotiators representing their own governments, and anonymous European brokers and middlemen who represented vague consortiums and conglomerates. Images of machine guns held aloft. Images of bidders consulting pocket calculators to determine the top prices they could offer. Images of flame-throwers and concussion grenades, of cluster bombs and Exocet missiles. Images of model jet fighters and helicopters on a scale of one inch to three feet. These were extravagantly detailed replicas; one of them even shot tiny pellets capable of breaching the skin. Images of land mines and torpedoes; images, at the far ends of the enormous room, of close-out bargains in obsolete hardware: bazookas, Browning automatic rifles, Colt .45s of interest to a small, nattering group of emerging nationals from Central America and the Near East. Images of a puffy, elegantly dressed salesman in a white suit and white Panama hat, long white cigarette holder and white cigarette, white shoes, holding a white piece of paper and addressing a group of black Africans, offering them "the very latest in personnel persuasion control equipment." Instruments of torture, Alec could see.

The noise level was terrific, the clicks of the hidden camera inaudible even to the photographer. Alec took half a roll, working his way toward the plump man in white. He was almost at point-blank range when his attention was abruptly diverted by an athletic figure dressed in the full military uniform of no known country. The beard and mustache deceived him at first, but nothing could disguise the high shoulders and the self-important gait. It was Ambassador Steelhead.

Alec followed him as the ambassador moved from table to table, handling and assessing the equipment. He asked prices, inquired knowledgeably about the velocity of missiles and the availability of rockets.

"And these?" He approached a table with model tanks.

"Very good. Very fresh. Just came in," said the proprietor. "Here. Take. Squeeze."

Steelhead picked up a large shell case. "How much?"

"Regular nine-dollar-fifty." By now Alec had learned that three zeroes were automatically added to any spoken price.

"Too much," Steelhead complained.

"For you, eight dollar seventy-five."

"Hey, Field Marshal. Big shot," a peddler screeched from his adjoining table. "I give to you cheaper. Eight-dollar-fifty."

Steelhead hesitated. His reply was lost in the competing cries of sellers and the grating of the crowd. Alec hoped that the tape recorder was sensitive enough to register individual voices. Steelhead moved on without buying anything.

He stopped at a small stand of grenades artfully arranged in pyramids. This was run by bright-faced chirping Orientals whose sign read: "No Connection With Reverend Moon." Alec stayed a little to the rear, blocked from view by a group of admirals furiously arguing the merits of a model submarine. Behind him a voice in English told them, "Buy now, gentlemen. I have another totalitarian, I can't mention his name, but his Swiss bank account is 591877761488, and he's willing to pay retail."

"When can you deliver?" One of the admirals held the submarine to the light and squinted at it.

"Well, gentlemen, you must realize we do quality checks, run innumerable immersion tests, do dry and wet runs, simulate battle conditions, have the test crew psychoanalyzed, make corrections within 0.1 micrometer of specifications—"

"We need by next Tuesday."

"You got it."

Smile and handshakes all around.

"No, no, gentlemen. You don't pay me now. I win it at the poker game. The girl at the register will give you details. The one at the six-weapons-or-less counter."

Alec turned his attention back to Steelhead. The ambassador was watching a peddler of warheads.

"Nuclear?" a customer was asking.

"No nuclear."

"Want nuclear."

"Whaddya want nuclear? This is just as good for a fraction of the price. And made right here in America. No Japanese material anywhere. I'll throw in a rebate."

"Too much cost."

"You got something to trade in?"

A pause for consideration. "An old tank division."

"How old?"

"Three years. But never used in a shooting war. Only to root out dissidents with rocks and bottles. A few dents is all."

"OK, I give 25 percent off."

"Plus rebate?"

The seller shrugged and hands were clasped in a pledge of lasting amity.

Alec recorded the exchange and took pictures of most of the exhibitors and their clients: the booth marked "Mishegunnah Martin: He Will Not Be Undersold," with its array of land and sea devices; the exhibits of radar and anti-aircraft shells; the lots of used and new smart bombs and tracer shells; the shelves of napalm and defoliation chemicals.

"Excuse me, sir." A small, white-gloved hand tugged at Alec's sleeve. He looked down at a tiny man in the formal whites of an unidentified navy.

"Jou to come with me."

Alec pulled his sleeve away. "I think you want somebody else."

But the little man grabbed his sleeve again. "Jou follow me."

"Sorry." Alec backed off.

"I am very persistent dwarf. The Hénéral, he says jou follow me."

"Hénéral Wolfe?"

"If jou say so."

"OK."

The little man made his way easily around or between the legs of the crowd. It took Alec a little longer. Out in the hall, the dwarf stopped at a door marked "Hallway to Exit," pushed the crash bar, and held the door open for Alec. Both men went through and the noise of peddlers and the throng of bidders was shut off. The hall was lit by a few 40-watt bulbs. Alec blinked in the dimness.

"Very good, Sixto." The voice was instantly recognizable.

I should have recalled, Alec thought. He always had Cuban help.

Gregory Ellenbogen winced as he separated the goatee and mustache from his supercilious face. "I suppose it was futile, but I had hoped we might be partners some day, Alec."

"Partners. I didn't even know you were alive. I saw your building collapse on television."

"You see talking rabbits on television. Do you believe them, too?"

"Those are cartoons."

"So is the news, Alec. That's what you and all the others fail to understand. A very costly error, if I may say. Kindly accompany me."

Alec looked around. Ellenbogen watched him. "Sixto is armed. So am I." Alec examined the little man's pistol. In his tiny grip it had a cannon effect. Alec walked up the echoing metal steps. Sixto indicated a small room marked "Custodian." He turned off the meager hall lights and opened the door. The three went inside. The place was illuminated by two long fluorescent cylinders designed to make people look like dybbuks.

"Please sit down." Ellenbogen perched on the side of the desk, making his thighs appear even wider under the white poplin. Alec took the only chair, a metal one with rubber casters.

Sixto leaned negligently against the wall. Ellenbogen said something to him in Spanish.

"The little man is in it with you, isn't he?" Alec asked.

"What little man?"

"The Mad Mosquito."

"Escudero? A greatly misunderstood maniac. Of course, like all terrorists he goes too far sometimes . . ."

"Like blowing up the Junta Verde embassy with my friend Crow in it?"

Ellenbogen merely shrugged. "An accident. Regrettable. You still don't understand any of it, do you? We don't espouse violence. We quell it. We're only here to give the world what it needs: stability."

"With guns."

"The world has tried everything else, Alec: negotiation, law, revolution. All quite useless. Arms may be noisy, but they produce quiet."

"Things don't seem very silent to me."

"Not now; not yet. But wait. Soon or late the oil will dry and the Third World will go back to sand and foliage. The biggest economies can collapse; neither the East nor the West may survive in their present forms."

"But you will."

"*We* will, Alec. The dealers. There will always be a garage sale somewhere."

"And an Ellenbogen to service it."

"Under some name or other. Ellenbogen is as good as any." He fondled the little Derringer in his palm. "I stole it, actually."

"The pistol?"

"The name. From a movie marquee. Associate producer. We once met. Mousy little fellow. But useful."

Alec wondered how long he would be required to stay

here, and when they would decide to kill him. There were only two exits: the door and the window, open from the bottom. When the curtains blew open they admitted gusts of wind and grit. Something got into Sixto's eye. He cursed and opened the window wider. He rubbed the corner of his eye with the pistol barrel.

"Use your handkerchief, for God's sake," Ellenbogen instructed the little man.

He explained to Alec: "I've tried to inculcate some basic manners in my staff. But they're only out of the trees one generation. Civilization takes time. And money."

Alec thought about money. He tried to remember how much insurance the network allotted him. Twice his salary, he recalled. Enough to take care of Azie for a while. Unless the cost of living kept encroaching.

"What are you thinking about?" Ellenbogen inquired idly.

"Interest rates."

"Yes, that would be like you."

Sixto was still rubbing his eye, this time with a piece of cloth last used for cleaning the barrel of his weapon. He put away the oily rag and turned to Alec. A large bluebottle fly came along and he gave that his attention. Ellenbogen continued:

"Alec, we simply can't have anybody tearing holes in the WEB. In a way my colleagues and I are delegates ourselves. From the Isles of the Opportune."

Sixto tried to swat the fly and missed. Ellenbogen shouted at him, but the little man stalked his quarry, now with a rolled-up copy of the *Afternoon Paper*. The headline read: "World on Brink."

"Be kind enough to rise and lace your fingers in back of your head," Ellenbogen said.

Alec tried to remember whether they were on the second or third floor.

"And we simply won't have you embarrassing our ambassador. It's not my decision. There are a lot bigger fish than me in this." Ellenbogen looked over the desk to see if he had left anything behind. Sixto swatted again, missed again, and refilled the air with yawps.

"Sixto, squash that insect this instant!" Sixto followed his chief's orders and left a dark stain on the wall.

"One keeps hearing about petrodollars." Ellenbogen's voice was suddenly theatrically calm. "Krugerrands, microchips, cocaine, and all the while the really big money is—"

But he got no further. Alec, at the doorway, clicked off the light. The room was in darkness except for a pale oblong of incandescence from outside the window. Alec dived for it. He clattered onto a rusty fire escape and righted himself. He could not tell which was louder, the feet behind him on the fire escape or the pumping of his heart.

In the city, evening was a relative matter. The flatulent air-conditioners raised the street-level temperature to noon highs. It was only slightly less bright than morning. High-intensity, crime-inhibiting lamps buzzed and radiated and the streets were visible to airplanes four miles overhead. Alec knew that it was impossible to vanish into the shadows; there were no shadows. A kneeling bus came by out of breath and chuffed to a stop. Alec boarded it before he realized that he had committed the most unpardonable urban crime: he did not have exact change.

"Out," ordered the conductor, scratching the boil scars on the back of his neck.

Alec regarded the blank, dissociated passengers. "Does anybody have change of a dollar?" They might have been George Segal sculptures. No one moved. He could hear steps back of him on the street. Alec turned to face two joggers, his saviors, dressed in midnight purple and bearing handfuls of tokens. Gratefully he traded in his paper money. A shower of coins sounded in the collection box. The driver closed the door, drove fifteen feet and stopped abruptly, hurtling Alec onto the lap of a sleeping woman with the face of a Notre Dame gargoyle. She twisted her moustache and growled. A cleaning lady, Alec guessed. Some day she and her colleagues would rise against him and demand the death penalty. He could hear their chants now. Or was it Sixto and Ellenbogen? Yes, there they were on the sidewalk, banging on the door, demanding admission.

The driver hesitated between the sadism of moving off without picking up passengers and the masochism of allowing new boarders on his cheerless vehicle. He sighed with his brakes, pushed a button, and opened the doors. As Alec's enemies entered the front of the bus, he exited the back. They ran shouting up the aisle, but by that time the back door had shut and the vehicle was in motion. Alec pounded on down the street until he came to a Food Emporium, open all night.

He moved through the aisles, past derelicts examining six-packs and couples searching for Perrier and limes. He found what he wanted on a back shelf, paid with a five dollar bill, and did not wait for change. In the doorway of Gay Rites, a shop offering children's collectibles, he ripped open his package. As the thirty-five–cent Woolworth dolls of the thirties, now priced at $150, stared blindly at him from the window, Alec pulled out that most ubiquitous symbol of New York and shook it out: a shiny black plastic garbage bag. It was the family size and by stepping in it very carefully he was able to pull it around him. He hopped, sack-race–style, to a group of similar plastic bags huddled and reeking at the curb. Ducking his head well in, he held the top closed with his fist.

It was a near thing; Sixto and Ellenbogen ran by a moment later, roaring in Spanish. Alec could not make out specific words but the tone was lethal. They were very close; he could hear a fat man's wheezing and a young man's curses. The sounds diminished and presently, disappeared. Alec, thinking of the Count of Monte Cristo dunked in the waters off the Chateau D'If, cut himself from the sack. "Rents are unreal," a cab driver explained to his fare as they passed Alec. "People will live anywhere." They sped on, heads shaking.

Now the only noise on the street came from a round hole. The end of a red metal ladder protruded from it, along with the sign: Persons Working. Evidently they were below the surface; no one was in the Con Edison truck. A white hard hat lay on the front seat. Alec reached inside, clapped it on his head, and lowered himself down the ladder.

A shower of sparks illuminated his descent. Three women were spot welding a joint of pipe and they were too concerned to notice their new neighbor. Gratefully he leaned against the tunnel wall and waited for an opportunity to regain the street. But just as the sparks stopped and one of the persons yelled, "Hey!" at him, another voice issued from an upside-down head at the manhole. It belonged to Sixto. Alec bolted for the open tunnel. Behind him came the persons, and behind them the dreaded pair.

Tiny incandescent bulbs showed a labyrinth of passages. An alternate and even gloomier Manhattan lay directly underneath the celebrated one. Alec moved swiftly, choosing the tunnels without thinking, dodging left, then right, then left again. Steps and shouts caromed around him. In six minutes Alec had gone from Edmund Dantes, the Count of Monte Cristo, to Jean Valjean moving through the miserable sewers of Paris. Now as he ran down a dingy subterranean path he thought of himself as Buster

Keaton in *Cops*, jerkily trying to escape the law in a black and white two-reeler. Except that the men tracking him were beyond the law. Abruptly he saw himself in *The Third Man*, as he had seen it once at Crow's.

"It's only the main sewer," the sergeant was saying. "Smells sweet, don't it?"

"I've been a fool," Trevor Howard murmured. "We should have dug deeper than a grave."

The signs blurred before Alec because of his speed and the constant frantic swiveling for a look backward. *We should have dug deeper than a grave.* I should have, anyway. Misdirection and shadows, Alec thought. I watched my father dupe the unsuspecting for years and here I am, the Master Gull, the All-Time Yuk. The Newsman as Victim. Worse, as collaborator. There were still some parts missing, but the shape of deceit was decipherable, the leads that were cul-de-sacs and the end that was really a beginning.

He looked not only for a way up but a way out. A small metal plate set into a pipe said 65th Street. An arrow pointed upwards. Dirty steel rungs were set in an outcropping of igneous rock. Above, hot water pipes snaked across the stone ceiling and steam escaped through holes in an iron square the size of a chessboard. Alec climbed up and pushed at the square. He had never known anything so small to be that heavy. But it came loose after the appropriate heaving and fulminations and he forced himself through the opening and out onto the street. Carefully Alec returned the plate to its proper place and stood upright, shaking.

"I used to live in there till it went condo." The voice was Hispanic, the weapon trained directly at Alec's stomach. But the man was only a derelict and he was only drunk and the gun was only a bottle of Danny Boy 5 Star muscatel. Too jarred to laugh, too weary to cry, Alec traded him a ten dollar bill for a quarter and tried to make a telephone

call. He tried nine times at nine different locations. In two
the wire had been severed by vandals. In the remaining
seven no dial tone sounded. All nine had been used as
urinals. With a rush of gratitude he recalled that this was
Mel's night at Tai Chi. Rose's husband would be away until at least midnight. Alec could make a house call. Rose
would help him decide the next move; she was a good
listener.

He worked his way to her apartment house, said hello
to the doorman who regarded him strangely—or was it
only Alec's fevered imagination? Yet the elevator man also
gave him a strange look. He rang the buzzer of 4B. There
were stirrings inside but he had to ring three times before
a voice mumbled indistinctly.

He identified himself and waved at the peephole.

Rose, dressed in a nightgown, opened the door a crack.
"Why are you wearing a hard hat?"

He took it off. "Because the sky is falling. It really is,
Rose."

"Go away."

"I need you."

"I have poison ivy."

'I don't need you for—where'd you get poison ivy?"

"From a poison ivy plant. Go away."

"I can't. Not until we talk." Alec felt fifteen years lift
away. He was a summer encyclopedia salesman again,
negotiating from the door, peering into the living room to
see if the slipcovers looked worn and whether there were
toys on the rug. People with children made the best pros-
pects.

"Why do all your books have dust jackets on them?"

"So they won't catch cold. Go away. Please!"

Sounds issued from inside, and at once Alec realized
that a day had dropped out of his life. This was not Thursday night, and Mel was not at Tai Chi.

"Who is it, duck?" inquired the heavy figure in blue pajamas.

"Trash no get collect tomorrow," Alec shouted. "Men go on strike."

"It's the super, lambie," Rose said over her shoulder.

"I go now." Alec backed away. "Don't forget. Mek plastic begs. Put outside in hallway. I collect tomorrow."

"Our super is from Donegal," she hissed.

"Is he now?" Alec assumed a brogue without missing a beat. "Then Oi'll be on me way. Ye'll remember to put it out in them big plastic bags now, not just scattered in the hall like ye usually do? There's been complaints about the coffee grounds and orange peels underfoot."

"What's wrong?" Rose asked. Then, louder to Mel: "It's just about the garbage."

Her husband answered hotly: "I'll give him garbage at this hour."

Alec backed off quickly. "I'm late for the IRA meetin'. Adoo to ye."

"Wait!" Rose shouted but her caller retreated down the hall until he came to the fire exit, glanced over his shoulder, and descended. The image he took away was of duck explaining things at the doorway while lambie scratched his big woolly head.

There were no cabs. He caught a crosstown bus, astonished to find it filled with passengers, and made his way to the back. Everyone in the bus seemed to be a relative of Sixto or Ellenbogen, but all of them avoided his eyes and assumed the posture and look, at once glazed and hostile, of the inner-city traveler.

He got off a block before the network building, patting the pockets where the devices were secreted. No one followed him. He stood at a corner pretending to examine the display of brassieres in a boutique, using the glass as a mirror to make certain that no one was approaching him from the back. His situation was not promising. Surely Ellenbogen and his friends knew that Alec had some sort of camera. They would be looking for him. Probably they had already staked out his apartment. Whether there were enough of them to watch the entrances of the network building was another matter.

There were. Approaching, he saw a long gray limousine with a television aerial on its roof. The General had a similar car, but his license was "Wolfe 1." This was a long number with a Z at the end: rented. Even from a distance, Alec could see the two men inside. Both were wearing fatigues; both stared with hostile dark eyes at the entrance.

Alec withdrew and worked his way around the block to the main doors. Another long limousine purred there, its air-conditioner and radio audible under the distant whines of ambulances and the metallic clang of trucks over manhole covers. Well, now he knew. It would be impossible to walk into the network. An attempt to run might be fatal. He thought briefly about the police, and dismissed the notion. The whole matter would take hours, even if they believed him. By now word about Alec's mission would be out, and the armory restored to its between-meetings emptiness. The photographs might provide evidence, but someone would have to develop and print them. The police would regard him as one more summer-evening nut. They might even impound his equipment. There was, of course, the General. . . .

The chief executive lived in the penthouse of Money Towers, a vast and secure structure only a few blocks from the WEB. Several network executives lived on lower floors; so did two best-selling novelists, four movie stars, a madam of international reputation, and many bi-coastal executives, industrialists, and hereditary heads of state. The emir had camped out here until he found his present digs. But the General strutted in the largest apartment, and the one with the best view. Alec had been there once, for a Christmas party. Wolfe had given a speech on integrity and sugar; all the cakes had been made of carob. Alec remembered the spectacular sunset and the sense of an eagle's nest. "Whenever I look out these windows," the General had informed his glazed listeners, "when I peer down at the world, I realize how small, how petty, our ambitions are." It was the kind of statement that could only be made by the occupant of the forty-seventh floor.

Alec walked in a circuitous and bizarre manner to Money Towers, glancing periodically over his shoulder or in the windows of shops. He could find no evidence of anyone remotely interested in his progress. At the apartment house he saw a ring of limousines, all of them empty, illegally parked but possessing Diplomatic or Press or Disabled license plates. Telephoning would be useless. The General had an unlisted number that was changed, to avoid calls from the sugar-crazed or the seekers of publicity, twice a day. Alec would have to trust to luck and timing. He approached the bright lobby, decorated in the neutral, foreboding tones of an airport, and entered. Immediately a large gristly man in a green and gray money-colored uniform approached. "Can I help you, sir?"

"I'm here to see General Wolfe." Alec spelled his own name and said that he was expected. The man disappeared to a recessed booth and called upstairs on a yellow house phone. Two other men with faces like Dobermans appraised Alec viciously. They had seen many gate-crashers in their years of service. But as the security guard returned from his booth their expressions relaxed to simple malignity.

"OK," the voice said. "Elevator three."

Another functionary in an identical uniform guided the elevator. "Face front," he snapped when Alec tried to comb his hair in a side mirror.

The elevator opened directly into the apartment. A sallow maid in black greeted Alec and brought him to the vast dark room where private guests were received. The ceiling, walls, and floor were mahogany; the oak bookshelves held 25,000 leatherbound scripts of every network show, from the Saturday morning cartoons to the most recent mini-series.

"Do sit down, Alger." The General extended a hand. He had appeared from behind a mahogany screen, holding a tired-looking volume.

"Story department still hasn't quite got it licked. No problem casting the Lilliputians, and we can always use special effects for the Brobdingnagians. And we can rotoscope the Houyhnhnms. But the Yahoos? Who could we possibly cast? I may have to abandon the whole idea. What do you think? Me, too."

"General—"

"You look agitated. A drink, perhaps. I thought so. I have some wine from a little vineyard I own near the Finger Lakes." He prattled on, pouring from a decanter and placing two ice cubes in the lead crystal glass. "Delicious, don't you think? I knew you would relish the secret sucrose-free blend." It had a turpentine aftertaste. The General sat in an ancient Barcalounger and made a conductor's motion to begin.

Alec knew that the General's attention span was only half the length of a commercial. He tried to be as terse as a station break, editing himself ruthlessly, excising details. The General seemed to follow, nodding, grunting from time to time. At several junctures a frown appeared and Alec thought he detected rapid eye movements of the sound sleeper, but the eyelids always managed to rise slowly, like curtains, and the shaved head gleamed in the light, nodding with a special vigor when Ambassador Steelhead's name was heavily and loudly dropped.

Alec had scarcely begun the part about Ellenbogen when General Wolfe broke in. "You go on the Morning Show with this," he said. "Taped. Unload your equipment. I'll call the technicians. We'll record you in the Presidents Room."

The Presidents Room: proof of Alec's significance. Nine national leaders had been invited to the ghastly magenta sanctum behind the Wolfe's dining arena. There, surrounded by glass-enclosed shelves containing rare morocco-bound transcripts of the Tonight Show, history had been made. Cameras had dutifully recorded the private, spontaneous, salty confidences of the great. These had been sharply and brilliantly edited to give the impression of coherence and intelligence. The place was lit with electric candles and at times it resembled a cathedral. That was understandable; the Presidents Room was one of the General's nondenominational holy places, second only to his anti-sugar room at the network where chemists worked to perfect liquors distilled from substances without sucrose. Currently they were trying to make something potable from okra; the pencil-shavings formula had not worked out.

Seated in a hard-backed deacon's chair, Alec was allowed to work on his notes, interrupted only once by Mrs. Wolfe, who wandered in by accident, stupefied with liquor.

"I love you," said the gorgon, shaking her magnificent head. Not an iron-gray hair fell out of place. The beautician had frozen them all with a spray customarily used on steel wool and tourists. Mrs. Wolfe advanced toward her victim with open arms. "You know why I love you? Because you're the one with the gin."

"No, no, pet," the General hastily interceded. "I said he's the one with the chin."

It took a few moments for the correction to register. "Chin?" she repeated piteously. The General responded

with a soothing voice and slow, reassuring movements.
With the help of a housekeeper, he guided his snuffling wife
away. Presently he returned to Alec. The incident with
Mrs. Wolfe might have been a public service announce-
ment; it had nothing to do with the scheduled program and
not a word was said about it. Instead, the General referred
to his notebook.

"I've sent for makeup, cameras, editors. Nap for a
while," he ordered. "It's going to be a long night, don't you
think? I agree."

Alec thought about power as the General withdrew.
How many people, in this town, at this time, can be summoned with a call in the night? The president had that kind
of sway and the heads of other states, and their advisers.
But no one could exert as much as the controller of a network. Politicians, military men, superstar athletes, movie
actors and directors, presidents of companies, psychia-
trists, professors would leave their desks and beds at an
instant if the General issued his famous summons.

The evening's anxieties and concerns crowded in upon
Alec. As he read, he found himself edging toward the border between fantasy and dread.

Corridors, explosions, threats jostled for attention.
Alec dreamed of Azie and mourned for Crow; he wondered
about his savage new brother Anthony and about the dot-
age of the Wizard. In the upper right-hand corner of his
mind's screen the Mad Mosquito capered and snorted. Accented voices challenged and bid in a clamorous hardware
market.

"15½ neck, 35 sleeve, right?"

It was a sour, sleepy messenger from Costumes. He
provided Alec with a new shirt and tie for the broadcast.
A dish-faced, aggressively cheerful woman from makeup
applied various powders and solutions. Alec went back to
his notes. The camera crew arrived and began setting up

the intricate machinery, checking lights and calibrating dials.

Alec excused himself and telephoned his father from the bathroom.

"Pop?"

"Alec?"

"News."

"Bad?"

"Good."

"Splendid!"

"Broadcast."

"When?"

"Tomorrow."

"Morning?"

"Watch."

"Certainly."

"Alec . . ."

"What?"

"Crow . . ."

"Yeah," Alec said, hanging up slowly. Crow would have liked it. He was big on newsbreaks. The only trouble was that in the end he was an innocent with no taste for vengeance. Well, Alec would compensate for him.

At 2:00 A.M. the broadcast was taped. Alec began with an observation by his favorite author: according to Halifax, he said, a man was easiest to trap when he was setting a snare for others.

And so it had proved, he told the camera. The arrogant merchants at the International Garage Sale were so busy enticing buyers of armaments, so certain of their immunity to prosecution, that they operated in an armory less than a mile from the World Body, a place where once the architects of peace had planned to eliminate war from the civilized vocabulary. Alec ran down his list of villains.

Stock footage of the World Body, still pictures that he had taken and that were now being developed, would be smoothly edited in by morning, the outrage carefully modulated by sound technicians. "The greatest shocker of all," Alec concluded, "was not the sale of arms. It was the participation of a public servant, an American"—he hesitated for emphasis—"a man so arrogant he barely bothered to disguise himself: Ambassador Lance Steelhead."

Alec let his report run for another three minutes, conscious that it was too long, but certain that the General, with his appetite for the sensational, would know what to leave in.

Not once did General Wolfe mention the name Grambling and, between takes, when the lighting was rearranged, he asked Alec, "Have you ever known a man to be hurt by a little desk experience? Neither have I." Alec took this to mean that after the broadcast, and the predictable hoo-ha, he would be elevated to a position at headquarters —possibly even to Grambling's job. He wondered what would happen to Grambling. Juneau bureau, probably. The tundra was where they sent news personnel on their way down; either that or the WEB. Well, that would change from here on. The WEB would be alive with investigative reporters. There would be charges and coverups and think-pieces. The *Morning Paper* would do several magazine articles on it, and on the vast white fields of their editorial pages, columnists would graze for months. Alec could already hear the thunderous bowel rumbles of the herd.

The taping was finished at 4:00 A.M. "Bit late," the General observed. "We'll order a limo."

Alec reminded the General that the network building

had been staked out. Surely someone would be watching his apartment. Wolfe, yawning widely, considered the alternatives.

"Outrageous that you should be kept from your bed by thugs. Still, alerting the police brings questions, reporters —and there goes our exclusive." He brightened. "Tell you what. "You'll sleep here. How about that? Not at all."

The General held up his hand to quiet Alec's protest. "We have twenty-two rooms; surely one of them will be to your liking. We'll put you up in the West Wing. Your choice of beds. They're all made. We never know who's going to drop in, do we? No."

A button was pushed and a small servant led Alec downstairs to the immense lower floor of the Wolfes' duplex. She handed him a towel and pointed down a long hall carpeted in rugs of exotic and memorable patterns. The colors were at once muted and warm; Alec had seen samples like these only in museums and once—where was it? Fatigue and the crowded day had worn out his memory.

He walked past a series of doors: the Presidential Room, the Senatorial Room, the Congressional Room, the Judicial Room, the Boom Boom Room; then a series of doors labeled with removable brass letters spelling the names of current network stars of dramas, comedies, and specials. There were no rooms commemorating journalists, although Alec could not help imagining one bearing his own name by next season.

He stood in the hallway, deciding which place to occupy for the remaining hours of the night; he would certainly be summoned for the 8:30 broadcast.

Maybe it was the hour, or his dwindling lack of judgment; perhaps it could be ascribed to some long-dormant curiosity. Whatever the reason, he decided that if there was a West hallway there must be a North, South, and East one, and he set out to explore them.

The other halls were more formal, the powerful rose-wood doors bearing brass plates with the names of bygone Americans: Charles Lindbergh, Douglas MacArthur, Theodore Roosevelt, Cecil B. De Mille. There was also a racketball court and a sauna.

Alec was about to turn back when he came upon the Billiard Room. He entered and inspected the bookshelves, filled with volumes obviously bought by the yard: unreadable matched sets of Harold Bell Wright, veterinarian encyclopedias long out of date, the memoirs of nineteenth-century robber barons and soldier-diplomats. Where large gaps occurred they were filled by foreign objects collected on the General's fact-finding trips: masks, fertility figures, keys to Kiev, Limoges, and Nutley, New Jersey; Eskimo sculpture; dolls, commemorative spoons; erotic netsukes; Frisbees from community colleges; and a large '30s radio in the shape of a cathedral. Alec turned it on and flipped the dial to an all-night Newark jazz station. Nothing came through but a hollow, amplified hum. He turned to the table, green and inviting as a meadow. It was lit by a conical lamp from above and, weary as he was, Alec decided to take a few shots before turning in. He closed the door behind him, selected a cue, chalked the tip, crooked his elbow on the felt and took aim. The shot missed. He climbed up on top of the green and bent over to make the next one.

The fine baize felt hot on his cheek, and the white cue ball seemed the earth itself, grown mute and lifeless. He had fallen asleep on the table and rested there—for how long? He consulted his watch. Five minutes to air time. His heart raced. Abruptly, laughter issued from some distant part of the room. It was metallic, cruel, and sustained. The chilly mirth was followed by dry coughing and sounds of a desk drawer opening and closing.

Alec got down from the table and looked around him. No one else was in the billiard room. The noise went on remotely, but now there were no human sounds. The live air and the crackles continued to reverberate; Alec traced them to the old radio. He turned the dial clockwise, but it had no effect. Neither did the volume control. He looked at his watch. There was no time left to puzzle over the radio. A large television set, also of ancient vintage, sat in a far corner. Alec went to it and turned the loose, rattling switch to On.

The set was a black and white model, dependent on tubes and welded circuitry. It took an eon to warm up and adjustments had to be made for the horizontal and vertical hold. Two anchorpersons emerged: Carole Drine and Rod Modell. It was the first time Alec had ever seen them in black and white; they looked like extras in a Don Ameche movie.

In another moment he himself materialized on videotape, the pale, jittery correspondent of a few hours ago in these very apartments. He broke the news of the International Garage Sale, the brazen trading of weapons and devices. Then he announced the great shocker: Ambassador Lance Steelhead, his country's representative at the World Body, was a buyer of armaments. The incriminating pictures appeared, poorly lit but unmistakable, the sound distorted but intelligible. What equipment the General must have at his disposal, Alec speculated; the state of the art was defined by this scandalous segment.

The footage came to a stop. The camera cut briefly back to Rod Modell. To his right was Ambassador Steelhead, live. The ambassador's eyes glistened with fatigue and resentment. They would be something in color. "I am grateful," Steelhead said, staring at the camera, "for this opportunity to refute these ridiculous and irresponsible charges. Yes, I was at the Garage Sale. But not as a customer or a seller. I attended as an observer. Here, look: I too had carried hidden cameras; I, too, bore miniature tape recorders."

As the set vibrated with Steelhead's protest a voice abruptly issued from radio. "The crisis is over," it said. "Steelhead is taking the fall. That füle from the network has done all our work for us. We meet in the delgates lounge at the üsual time." Sounds of movement occurred, then silence.

Someone with large hands rapped on the door three times. Alec ran to the old radio, loosened a tube, and told him to come in.

"Ah," the General said. "There you are! Saw the show from in here, eh? What did you think? Devastating."

"Revealing."

"Want a game of billiards after breakfast? Glad to oblige."

"I could use some coffee." Alec joined his employer at the door, speaking fluently as he went. He was anxious to leave the billiard room, to go somewhere, anywhere, and plan his next move. He was certain now: the radio was no radio at all. It was part of a hookup connecting the General and Bjørn Gruner, Secretary of the World Body. *There are a lot bigger fish than me in this,* Ellenbogen had said. Those two sharks, and who knew how many others, were the real operators of the Garage Sale. The ambassador, the pompous, humorless, blundering Lance Steelhead, lover of Gomer Pyle and Third World oratory, was innocent, railroaded because of Alec's efforts. Alec blushed at his lethal innocence. Same old Alec; all the time he thought he was acting on his own, he had been on stage providing misdirection while the operators put over the biggest con of his time.

11

The General held a telephone in his fist, nodding vigorously, his head gleaming in the track lights. "He's debriefing now. Absolutely not." He hung up.

"Requests for your appearance on talk show. Also a publisher wants to see you about writing a book."

When Alec began to speak the General broke in with reassurances: "It's making a *habit* of books that I find counter-productive. The occasional well-reviewed best-seller never did anyone any harm. You'll use Joseph Ebbing. He ghosted the president's book on the decline of integrity. And he wrote mine on broadcast ethics. You just talk into a tape recorder and six months later there's your book."

"General Wolfe," Alec stared out with sleepless eyes, "I didn't really rest very well last night."

"Of course, strange surroundings, deadlines. We'll set you up in better digs tonight. Perhaps the General MacArthur Room? Excellent."

"My own place will do. I—"

"Wouldn't take the chance. Never know about terrorists. Wait a few weeks. There'll be a Senate investigation starting Friday, and a complete restructuring of our delegation. All thanks to you. This is large. Oversized. Historic. I see an Emmy in this, maybe even a Movie of the Week."

He scattered names and places, promising fresh assignments, endless foreign and domestic travel, celebrity, Alec's name in textbooks.

Alec frantically recalled that although there were no little Wolfes, each year the General gave a vast Christmas party for the children of employees. There, amid the consumption of nauseating sugarless cake and the presentation of breakable plastic replicas of the network building, he would bombinate about the value of innocence in a corrupt world.

Alec interrupted his chief's invitation. He stressed Azie's inability to understand her father's sudden prominence, how she would have to hear from him personally, the value of face-to-face contact. "We were thinking," he lied, "my wife and I . . . times like these . . . daughter . . . mere child . . . tears . . . marriage counselor . . . possibility of getting together again. . . ."

The General's impartial expression melted. "Of course, of course. A conjugal visit. By all means. Take two hours. Three. Bring flowers. I'll send for roses. You're welcome."

Alec protested, but the General would brook no more interruptions. A bouquet was delivered, the refrigerated white box placed in Alec's hands. He went off with Brogan, the bodyguard-chauffeur whose instructions were: not, under any circumstances, to let this most valued employee out of his sight. It was all going according to plan, Alec saw —the General's plan. Even his escape from Ellenbogen had been planned, he realized. He was *supposed* to dive out the window and down the fire escape. No wonder he had no trouble eluding his pursuers. It had all been staged as neatly as the network's special on the Pentagon.

He and Brogan stopped for beer in a bodega just around the corner from Laura's. As they approached the lobby Alec prayed that Azie and Laura would be home. Or the cleaning lady. Anybody. He leaned hard against the bell and almost instantly the voice sounded.

"It's Alec," he shouted. "I'll explain later."

"Explain now," said Laura's disembodied voice.

"Didn't you see the Morning Show?"

"The set's busted."

Alec addressed the metal plate with its circle of holes as if it were an intimate of many years. He put his hand on it and spoke in pleasant, unconcerned tones as his brain boiled.

"Is Azie home?"

"Yes. She has a little cold."

"Probably an allergy."

"I'll call Dr. Schwartz. Well, good-bye."

"Laura!"

Evidently the distress in his voice traveled upward even on that primitive device. The buzzer sounded, admitting him and his glowering companion. He motioned Brogan into the elevator first, but the bodyguard shook his head. "I'm not supposed to let you outa my sight. Even inna crapper."

Introductions were perfunctory. Laura offered them coffee; Alec displayed the six-packs along with the flowers.

"At eight-thirty in the morning?"

"Best thing."

Brogan agreed and they sat at the kitchen table, sipping directly from cans while Laura fetched her daughter.

"Hi, Daddy," she said, sniffling. "You can smell the flowers all the way down the hall. I just heard about you on the news."

"Your father is already semi-famous," Brogan informed her.

At this Laura perked up. Alec modestly dismissed his achievement, then Azie gave her version. "They were selling guns at the World Body and Ambassador Steelhead is going to resign and Senator Bland is going to have an investigation. All because Daddy blew the whistle on them."

"It took tremendous guts." Brogan belched loudly.

"Speaking of tremendous guts," murmured Azie.

Alec sipped at his beer as his daughter, with large, devouring eyes, watched Brogan consume four.

Alec asked for her notebooks and pretended to examine them, but the pictures of the solar system dissolved into meaningless patterns.

"Imagine that," Alec commented blankly. "There are nine planets. What won't they think of next?" He kept babbling until Brogan asked for the bathroom. The bodyguard stood, pondering. "They didn't say nothing about you being there when *I* go." He stumbled off.

Alec looked at Laura. "Quick: do you have trouble sleeping?"

"Occasionally," she replied defensively. "I don't see that it's—"

"Just want to know if you have any Seconal."

"One or two?"

"Take them all and dump them into the next can of beer he asks for."

"It'll kill him."

"Not Brogan."

"Alec—" They heard the sound of water running.

"Life and death," he urged.

When Brogan reentered, Alec was morosely examining the orbit of Uranus. "I tell you what." He brightened. "Let's play Monopoly."

Azie reminded him: "You told me it encouraged greed."

"Greed is holistic," Alec said between his teeth. "There was a thing about it in the *Morning Paper.*"

Azie gave him a dark sideways look but she brought the board and pieces. Laura presented her guest with a fresh beer. All four of them played, purchasing properties and utilities, vying with each other for possession, and crowing when a card turned up a rich relative or the dice rolled doubles. Two hours later, shortly after he had advanced to St. Charles Place, Brogan showed the first signs of disinterest: he refused another can when it was offered. Shortly afterward he confused Ventnor with Tennessee Avenue, then with the Water Company, and finally with a piece of toast.

"Time for my exercise." Abruptly dropping to the floor, Brogan did forty-eight pushups. "One for each year," he grunted.

"Wouldn't you be more comfortable with your jacket off?" Laura asked.

"I would, thank you. But I don't want to frighten the child." He stopped exercising long enough to whisk his lapel back, revealing a dark leather shoulder holster.

"Shawna's mother has one of those," Azie said. "She carries it in her bosom. Everybody thinks it's silicone."

But Brogan was not listening. He had become fascinated with the kitchen floor.

"The pattern on your linoleum looks like my sheets," he said, closed his eyes, and slept.

Alec raised his hand, calling for silence. Breathing slowly through their mouths, Laura and Azie looked down at the lumpish form, twitching occasionally like a Central Park carriage horse, as he began to snore with reassuring sonority.

"What if the linoleum had looked like his shower curtain?" Azie whispered. Alec raised his fingers to his lips and signaled to his ex-wife and his daughter to follow him down the hall, and out the door. Brogan's slow, machine-like exhalations were audible in the hall, and Alec thought he could hear them out on the street, like disembodied effects from Poe.

"*Now* will you tell me—" Laura began, but Alec would not talk then, nor on the trip downtown to the rent-a-car place, nor in the Ford Escort, not until they had passed into

Connecticut. Silently he drove, his eyes repeatedly glancing up to the rearview mirror.

"We just went across the state line," Laura informed him. "This constitutes kidnapping."

Azie, who regarded the morning as the best and most eventful since Shawna was groped by an associate producer, had never been happier. The motion of the car relaxed her and she, too, slept with a wide, satisfied grin.

"All right. I'll try to explain." Alec kept driving, but he relaxed his grip on the steering wheel. He described his night, ending in the billiard room. Laura was too absorbed in the narrative to comprehend the punch line. "I knew the voice after the first umlaut," he said.

"I don't quite . . ." Laura responded.

"It was Gruner. The secretary-general. Don't you see? He's the one I should have been after. Steelhead really *was* trying to expose the Garage Sale. All along, ever since I was assigned to the WEB, I've been programmed to snare the wrong man. To take everybody's eyes off Bjørn Gruner."

"Who by?"

"Wolfe. And all the other weapons dealers."

"The *Gen*eral?" Laura shook her head. "Impossible. He already has nineteen drillion dollars and all the power."

"There's power and Power. He can control who reports the news, but he can't control events. Not without hardware he can't. So he makes sure the arms get in the proper hands. A junta here, a revolution there. Doesn't matter where, doesn't matter who."

"But he must be on somebody's side."

"Not him. He has no ideology. He doesn't believe in anything. None of them do. Except stability. As long as who's on top stays on top: radicals, militia, emperors, anybody. It's a nice tight organization and I was one of its best soldiers. Well, I'm discharged. Here: souvenirs."

"What are these?"

"Stuff from my own backup system." He produced a small roll of film and a cassette no larger than a matchbook. "In case their camera and recorder didn't work."

"Alec, you can't drive away now. You've got to show these to people. Go on the air with them."

"Who would watch? Who would listen? The World Body is the greatest fiction of our time. Everybody believes it prevents war. On the front steps they have a statue of a peacemaker beating a sword into a plowshare. Attack the WEB, you melt down that statue. You burn the Bible."

"But you've got to release these things," Laura insisted. "Besides, it's dangerous to hold on to them. If anyone ever finds out—"

"Nobody'll find out."

"But if they do . . . Oh, Alec, you'll have to move to another planet."

"Where we're going is just as far."

The fieldstone buildings warmed in the late March sun. A few sulphur butterflies, deceived by the surge in temperature, whirled around the green, searching vainly for petunias. The sounds of an acoustic guitar, played with fervor but little skill, were accompanied by a small true voice wailing of cannons and petals.

The students for History and Literature I shifted and palavered restlessly. The professor was ten minutes late. It was unlike him. But, as it happened, just as he had gathered his notes and prepared to leave his office he had been confronted by a businessman, choleric under his tan, dressed in a Paul Stuart three-piece flannel suit and matching toupee.

"Everyone understands," the man said with some asperity.

"By everyone you mean the General."

Grambling ignored the reply. "He isn't even mad about all the letters you returned. Without even opening them, for Chrissake. You were trying to get your life together—very nice about you and Laura, by the way. You were exhausted. You needed a sanctuary. He's very simpatico. Really. News is allowed two burnouts per fiscal quarter." He looked around at the old stucco faculty buildings. "Not exactly one of your Big Ten," he said derisively.

"Only two channels up here," Alec agreed. "The network comes in fuzzy. Of course in a way it always did."

"Look, Alec—"

"Matter of fact, the local channel's on campus right now. The Spring Carnival piece."

"I know. I saw the sound truck. You can't get away from TV, Professor. Why do it for free? Come on. The General misses you. *I* miss you, you old fox." He gave Alec a playful rabbit punch in the neck.

"He just wants to keep an eye on me," Alec said.

"Well, that too. But think of the perks."

"I'd rather be here. Tell the General he has nothing to worry about."

"Don't you think he knows that? Listen, you get a 30 percent salary raise plus stock options. Title of News Editor."

"But that's your job."

"Was. I'm getting London Bureau Chief. Everybody wins, Professor. Come on, rest period is over. Finish out the term, no rush. Then come on back to the real world. Everybody wins," he repeated.

"Looks like it," Alec answered. And so it did.

Senator Bland won, presiding over the hearings with great rectitude and personal style, his reelection certain. Not since Claude Rains closed Rick's Place ("I am shocked,

shocked to find gambling going on in here"), while pocketing his winnings, had any figure spoken so convincingly of turpitude. Before his drawl, vice consuls and former advisers—for they had all resigned—withered. "The days of Garage Sales are at an end," he boomed directly into the camera, and that night Americans slept better.

So did the emir, exothalmic eyes shut, toy missile held firmly in his mouth, along with a teddy bear's ear. Tomorrow in the desert, the emir's armies would receive real missiles with authentic warheads. It was expensive, he thought dreamily, but worth every tankerful of oil. And he would economize from now on. His wives would fly tourist class.

It would not be correct to say that Maurice Damar slept better. He seldom slept at all. High on cocaine, the first Arab standup comedian had become a sensation; the overnight Neilsens had given him a 43 percent share of the audience. Commuters and students repeated his yocks and boffeaux: "I just bought my wife a mink outfit: a rifle and trap"; "I solved the parking problem—I bought a parked camel." "I will never forget my schooldays. I was teachair's pet. She could not afford a dog."

Anthony preferred not to sleep. The streets were so different from the dirt bullock tracks of his childhood that after he had been tucked in he crept down hallways and fire stairs in order to enjoy the evening life of the city: the pornography, the tourists with their carelessly open purses and jackets, the stolen goods he peddled so easily from doorways. But his new mother Lenore slept well. The Women's General Strike was now in its seventh month. True, most of the women had returned to work, or to their homes, and in fact no more than 8 percent had ever participated. Nevertheless, the principle was alive and she had moved to new headquarters in a rebuilt structure in the

East Sixties. The landlord had been reluctant to discuss the previous tenants, but she learned, much to her pleasure, that the Junta Verdeans had been on this very floor. Fitting, she wrote in her diary, that the downtrodden should follow each other in real estate as in history.

The General, Bjørn Gruner, and five of their associates from Africa, Asia, and Europe slept lightly in their box seats in the darkened arena of Carnegie Hall as a succession of opera stars, rock groups, Hollywood celebrities, and politicians performed on behalf of the Committee for Bilateral Disarmament. Later, there would be an auction for the cause. The men in the boxes would donate identical rugs, presented to them by the emir.

Rose began sleeping for two. After years of informing their friends, "I wouldn't bring kids into this mess," Mel decided that he wanted a child after all, in case the nuke business was only a lot of smoke.

Ram Pandit, at loose ends, visited Radio City Music Hall for the first time. He fell instantly and tumultuously for the chorus line: twenty-two girls—or, as he saw it, forty-four legs. He treated the line not as a series of individuals but as an entity, writing it notes, sending it flowers, dreaming of a godlike consummation.

"Pop?"
"Alec!"
"OK?"
"Fabulous."
"Really?"
"Rich!"
"You?"
"Yep!"
"Vegas?"

"No."
"Atlantic City?"
"No."
"Catskills?"
"No."
"Where?"
"Here!"
"Magic?"
"No."
"How?"
"Blackmail."
"W-who?"
"Sleep—"
"But—"
"—tight."
"Pop!"
"Zzzzz."
Click.

The Mad Mosquito seethed. Imagine paying out so much dinero to the Wizard. What could that silver-haired hyena prove? How much could he possibly know? Admittedly, Escudero had been at many places that blew up afterward. But coincidence was not enough to convict in a court of law; not in this country. What kind of world was it where magicians could not be taken care of with gelignite? Still, the Mosquito was a good soldier; his country's new image was non-violence, its new shibboleth passive resistance. All embassy employees had to trade in their Genghis Khan buttons for Mother Teresa bumper stickers. He made his peace with it. He stayed home at night and fell asleep watching S and M movies on his Betamax. But he slept with his rifle under his mattress. Regimes altered, orders changed. Years in the mountains had taught him that.

The colonels paused to examine the fresh gold lettering on the door: Truth Well Told.

"Come in!" The shout was bracketed by coughs. The colonels entered and watched the speaker drain the last of his vodka from a white plastic coffee cup.

"You are Hackett the journalist?" one of them asked.

"No longer, my friend. I'm into something clean now. International public relations. Your names in ink: bloodless coup . . . welcoming throngs . . . experienced hands at the helm . . . new realities . . . free elections within a year. . . ."

The colonels exchanged glances. They had not been misinformed. Here, clearly, was that rarest item, a useful American.

One of the colonels reexamined the door. "How much is the cost of truth?"

"It's a priceless gem, gentlemen, priceless." Nevertheless he consulted a price list.

"Quickly, man. We have no time to haggle. We have to condemn the West in twenty minutes."

"I'm only taking this because of my affection for the Third World," Hackett said. "My ex was from the Third World. I always marry them, you see."

As he started to describe his glandular replacement they settled on a sum. After his new clients left, Hackett slept, smiling, with his head on the *Afternoon Paper*, obscuring the headline: "Global Rape."

But the students of Literature and History I were not allowed to sleep. For one thing, they were too curious about the large camera in the back of the room with the call letters WBX across it, and the fat, blasé cameraman chewing a dead cigar. Professor Alec Lessing, in his new kinetic style, kept moving around the classroom, shouting phrases and challenging his listeners. Even Grambling, sitting in the back row, under orders not to leave the campus without Alec's consent to return, was unable to shut his eyes. Afterwards, with charts, he would show Alec the folly of raising a family on an assistant professor's salary. Probably the sound man made more than Alec did. Grambling's mind, restive when far from the editing room and the amiable chatter of teletype machines and anchorpeople, was trying to wander when Alec brought it back.

The professor was writing something on the blackboard. Grambling could make out the name Karl Marx without his glasses. Surely Alec had not become a Red. He wiped his bifocals and read the sentence in quotes: "History occurs twice—the first time as tragedy, the second as farce."

"Can anyone explain?" In his mind Alec could still see the boy dressed as the American flag writing that phrase back at Princeton, on another blackboard in a time as remote as the Stone Age.

There were no replies. Frowning faces and averted eyes greeted Alec's glance. He looked at Grambling and thought of the terrorists and of General Wolfe and his network. He thought of the hazards of power and the safety of obscurity. He thought about the International Garage Sale and of what happens to those who inquire too closely. He thought of Azie and Laura. He thought of the World Body. And he remembered Crow.

And then he took a deep breath and looked at the camera and told them what Marx meant.